"I don't exp
to know, but you don't have any responsibility, here. You're free to go on with your life as if Josh and I don't exist."

Gage stared at her. "Are you kidding?"

"Not at all." Emma's expression gentled. "You didn't choose this, Gage. I don't want to saddle you with a child you never intended to create."

"You didn't choose this either."

"Not initially, but after I made my decision, I never looked back. I haven't regretted it for one second. You had no say, though. Expecting you to adjust your life to fit a choice I made is unfair."

He met her gaze. "I don't know what's fair or unfair. This is all so…"

"You're still in shock."

"Yeah." He scrubbed a hand through his hair. "That about sums it up. I need some…time."

She nodded.

"But I can tell you one thing."

"What's that?"

"I could never go on with my life as if you and Josh didn't exist."

A COWBOY'S BABY

THE MCGAVIN BROTHERS

Vicki Lewis Thompson

Ocean Dance Press

A COWBOY'S BABY
© 2018 Vicki Lewis Thompson

ISBN: 978-1-946759-57-3

Ocean Dance Press LLC
PO Box 69901
Oro Valley, AZ 85737

Cover art by Kristin Bryant

Visit the author's website at
VickiLewisThompson.com

Want more cowboys? Check out these other titles by
Vicki Lewis Thompson

The McGavin Brothers
A Cowboy's Strength
A Cowboy's Honor
A Cowboy's Return
A Cowboy's Heart
A Cowboy's Courage
A Cowboy's Christmas
A Cowboy's Kiss
A Cowboy's Luck
A Cowboy's Charm
A Cowboy's Challenge
A Cowboy's Baby

Thunder Mountain Brotherhood
Midnight Thunder
Thunderstruck
Rolling Like Thunder
A Cowboy Under the Mistletoe
Cowboy All Night
Cowboy After Dark
Cowboy Untamed
Cowboy Unwrapped
In the Cowboy's Arms
Say Yes to the Cowboy
Do You Take This Cowboy?

Sons of Chance
Wanted!
Ambushed!
Claimed!
Should've Been a Cowboy

_1_

"So that's the story." Gage Sawyer glanced over at his brother Wes as they sat at one of the little bistro tables in Pie in the Sky. "She shot me down. I'm embarrassed to tell you about it. Probably wouldn't except I figured I had to after I let you in on my grand plan to go see her."

"I hate that it turned out that way." Wes sighed. "Did she give you any encouragement at all?"

"Not an ounce." He took a swig of his double-shot latte. The bakery had stopped serving the triple-shot Firecrackers at the end of July or he would have ordered one of those. "Said she was sorry I'd driven all the way up to Great Falls for nothing, closed the door in my face and locked it. Doesn't take a genius to get that message."

"Guess not."

"It appears that nineteen months is too long to go without contacting a woman. Who knew?"

"Probably depends on the woman."

"Or the man." He scowled at his brother. "Wore my lucky hat, too. I clearly overestimated my manly appeal yesterday."

Wes pushed the plate of brownies in Gage's direction. "Are you gonna have any of these?"

He shook his head. "Thought I would when I ordered them, but reliving that fustercluck has ruined my appetite."

"I'm not letting them go to waste, then." Wes picked up a brownie and bit into it.

"Go right ahead." He stared out the bakery display window at the folks walking along Main Street enjoying the beautiful fall afternoon. "You know what makes it suck even worse?"

"She's prettier than you remember?"

"She is, as a matter of fact, but that's not what sticks in my craw." He turned back to his brother. "She wasn't even mad. If she'd yelled at me and slammed the door, then I'd have figured maybe groveling would make a difference. Instead she quietly closed and locked it, like I was some annoying salesman."

Wes chewed and swallowed. "I hate to say it, bro, but—"

"Don't say it. I get the picture."

"What now?"

"I see several longnecks in my future."

"You didn't get that out of your system when you came home last night?"

"Oddly enough, I did not. Just didn't appeal to me."

Wes eyed him across the table. "Whoa, this is serious. I've never known you to be too discombobulated to drink a beer."

"I was then, but not anymore. Walking into town just now helped."

"You *walked* here?"

"It was only about four or five miles."

"I've never known you to walk even one mile."

"Me, either, to be honest. I don't intend to make a habit of it, but the exercise mellowed me out some. My feet hurt, though. I should've worn those gym shoes I bought for flag football but then I'd be walking around town in gym shoes looking dorky."

"I'll give you a lift back."

"Appreciate it. I need to fetch my truck, anyway. I'm thinking I'll head to the Guzzling Grizzly tonight. It's Friday. Bet I could find some single ladies who are in the mood for dancing."

"You just might."

"You and Ingrid want to join me? I promise to be the life of the party. Hangdog is not a good look on me."

Predictably, a mention of Ingrid had his brother glancing past the bakery case to the open kitchen where his blond sweetheart was kneading bread dough. He was twitter-pated over that lady. Gage was jealous of his happiness but pleased for him, too, if that made any sense.

Wes was smiling like a love-struck teenager when he turned around again. "I'll ask her, but we can't stay long. She has to get up at three in the morning."

"I keep forgetting that. But you could at least have dinner, take a few turns around the dance floor. Don't want to let yourself get rusty. The Sawyer men have a reputation to uphold, you know."

He grinned. "Then you'd better inform Pete of that fact. I can't remember the last time he went dancing."

"Good point. I'll drag him along tonight, too."

"Sounds like a plan." Wes looked over at his sweetie again. "I'll ask her once she gets that bread in the oven. I'll bet she'll want to go."

"'Course she will." He picked up his coffee mug. "I need to put a shine on my dancing boots. Mark my words, this ol' boy is gonna..." He lost track of what he'd been about to say as a familiar scent drifted his way. His back was to the door so he couldn't see who had just come through it, but nah, couldn't be who'd popped into his mind.

"Could you please tell me where I can find Gage Sawyer?"

He froze. *No way.*

Clearly she hadn't noticed him sitting there, which gave him a moment to collect himself. Meanwhile Abigail, the bakery's owner, was hedging, politely inquiring how she knew Gage. *Thank you, Abigail.*

Wes leaned forward and lowered his voice. "Do you know her?"

"Sure do." Gage carefully put down his coffee mug. "That's Emma."

Wes's eyes widened. "Well, she's not alone."

"A guy?"

"A baby."

His body jerked as if he'd grabbed a frayed electrical wire. His vocal cords tightened as he stared at his brother. "*A baby?* How old?" His heart was thumping super loud, but not loud enough to block out Emma's voice as she talked with Abigail.

Wes glanced toward the counter. "Might be a year or so, give or..." His attention swung back to Gage and he hunched over the table. His lips barely moved. "Could it be yours?"

"No." Gage's jaw clenched. "I always used a—"

"I believe you. FYI, they're leaving."

"Can't have that." Snatching his hat off the table, Gage stood and faced the door. "Emma."

She stopped in mid-step. The baby peered over her shoulder and looked straight at him.

Holy shit. The blond hair was all Emma, but the big brown eyes were the same ones that gazed out from every picture of him at that age. His stomach bottomed out. He hadn't looked at the old albums in years, but he didn't need to. This was his kid.

His kid. He fought panic. *His kid!* Yet how in the hell....

Emma turned slowly. So did the little guy, twisting in her arms while he focused on Gage with the intensity of a gunslinger at high noon. Cold sweat trickled down Gage's spine.

She said nothing, just stared, skewering him with her green eyes. Clearly she was once again taken aback by his sudden appearance, but today there was a subtle difference. She looked...prepared. She had on makeup. "Where's your truck?"

"It's not..." He paused to clear his throat. It was the only sound in the bakery. Abigail, Ingrid and half-a-dozen customers stood in suspended animation, like figures in a wax museum. "It's...not here."

"I know. That threw me off."

He'd thrown *her* off?

"Gage, we need to talk."

He gulped. "I can see that."

She adjusted her hold on the baby and grabbed at the strap of a small purse dangling from her other shoulder. "Privately."

"You can go up to my apartment." Wes's chair scraped against the floor as he stood. "That's handy."

Gage sent him a quick glance. "Thanks, bro. Much obliged." He damn near asked Wes to come along. As a referee.

Wes dug in his pocket, pulled out a key and handed it over. "Take all the time you need. Help yourself to...oh, wait, there's not much in the fridge. Or the cupboards, for that matter. There's water."

"It's okay." Gage struggled to breathe normally. "I can...I don't need—" Oxygen would be good. He could use a tankful of that.

"Take the brownies."

"Yeah." He picked up the plate so fast he had to tip it quick or the brownies would've hit the floor.

Emma frowned. "Where is this apartment?"

"Over the bakery." Gage moved closer, but he was hesitant to get in her space. Or even more scary, in the kid's space. Yesterday she'd given him the bum's rush. Today she was the mother of his son. Crazy didn't begin to cover it.

"'Scuse me." He scooted around her so he could hold the door. "It's this way. I'll be right behind you."

The baby's unblinking gaze continued to track him as Emma carried him through the doorway and out to the sidewalk. Then the little guy bounced in her arms and gave him a grin that revealed four teeth, two on the top and two on the bottom. "Da-da!"

Gage almost passed out.

"He calls everyone that, including me."

"How...confusing."

"He's eleven months old. He has no idea what it means."

"Right." Stepping outside, he let the door swing shut. "Over here." He started toward the outside entrance to the upstairs apartments. Then he nearly dropped the brownies again as he fumbled with the key. *Get it together, Sawyer.*

After he opened the door, she walked past him trailing a sweet, flowery scent that brought back those hot December nights in her bed. Which time had the condom failed to do its duty? They'd been fresh from the pharmacy, damn it. A reliable brand. *A baby. Dear God, he had a baby.*

After glancing up the stairs, she snugged the little boy in tighter and began the climb.

His manners kicked in. "Would you like me to carry—"

"I've got him."

"Okay." He was in no rush to make contact. The way his hands were sweating he might drop him.

He followed her up. Her taffy-colored hair had been loose yesterday, but today she'd gathered it back with a silver clip. The baby stared over her shoulder, keeping tabs on him. "Go right at the top of the stairs. First door. Should be open."

"Thanks." She was puffing a little.

"How much does he weigh?"

"Twenty-six pounds."

His baby weighed twenty-six pounds. What else should he ask? Oh, yeah. "What's his name?"

"Josh."

"Short for Joshua?"

"No, just Josh."

He'd never known a Josh. He didn't hate the name. He could get used to...wait. Kids usually got two names. He was Gage Brendan, after an uncle he hadn't seen in years. What if she'd used Gage? Josh Gage sounded weird. "What's his middle name?"

"Preston."

Preston? "Why?"

"My dad's name."

News to him. "Do your parents know?"

"Of course."

Naturally. Her folks, who'd moved to Green Bay, Wisconsin, years ago partly because they liked being the Greens from Green Bay, were now grandparents. She would have informed them, even if she'd decided not to tell him.

The door to Wes's apartment was not only open, but ajar. She walked in and he followed.

She surveyed the living room where nothing was out of place. Even the navy-blue throw pillows on the beige sofa were perfectly arranged. "I can't believe someone actually lives here."

"Mostly Wes is at his girlfriend's. Go ahead and sit wherever you want."

"Thanks." She chose the sofa and struggled to keep Josh on her lap as he crowed happily and strained to reach the plate of brownies Gage was holding.

"Does he want one of these?"

"Oh, he sure does. But in nothing flat he and I would both be wearing it. We'd need to be taken out back and hosed down."

"Then I'll make them disappear." Carrying the plate into the kitchen, he stuck it on a shelf in the mostly empty fridge. The cold air felt good. He breathed in a few lungsful.

When he returned to the living room, Emma had put Josh down. He was slowly working his way around the coffee table, his steps determined, his concentration intense.

Gage followed his progress, mesmerized by each wobbly step taken in impossibly tiny gym shoes. His baby was almost walking. His wispy blond hair had a slight curl to it, like Emma's.

"He still needs to hold onto something. But soon he won't have to."

He glanced over at her. She was watching the baby as intently as he was.

Just then the little guy lost his balance. He sat down with a soft thud and a very adult-sounding *oh.*

"Whoops." Gage started toward him, ready to help.

"Let him do it."

"But—"

"This table is a lot like the one I have at home. He can get back up."

Sure enough, the kid shifted to a crawling position, motored back to the table leg and used it to haul himself upright again.

"Smart little guy."

"Oh, yeah. I've baby-proofed the heck out of my house and he still gets into things."

"Were you ever going to tell me?"

Her expression grew wary. "Well, I..." She paused and drew in a shaky breath. "Would you please sit down?"

"Okay." He took the easy chair since he figured she'd rather have him there than cozied up next to her on the sofa. Laying his hat on the arm of the chair, he sat back and waited.

Instead of looking at him, she focused on Josh. "I kept meaning to call you. Well, after I faced the fact I was pregnant."

"I swear I'd just bought those condoms."

"I know. I was the one who opened the box, remember?" She gave him a quick glance before returning her attention to Josh. Her cheeks were pinker than they'd been a moment ago. "It was a fluke."

"Yes, ma'am." Evidently discussing their former sexual activities got to her. It got to him, too, but he'd keep a lid on it. Her first reaction to seeing him again had spoken louder than words. "You still had my number?"

"I never deleted it from my phone. At first I put off calling you because I was in denial. Then I couldn't figure out what to say. In the end, I decided you'd be better off not knowing. You didn't seem like the daddy type, so why throw a monkey-wrench into your life when I didn't expect to ever see you again?"

"And you didn't. Until yesterday."

Turning her head, she met his gaze. "We'd agreed we were just having fun, nothing serious."

"True." Yet those nights with her stood out in vivid detail all these months later. "So if I hadn't come to see you yesterday..."

"You'd be none the wiser."

His chest tightened. Finding out about Josh had knocked him six ways to Sunday, but never finding out....

"Anyway, you did come to see me."

"And you told me to leave."

"I wasn't prepared. I panicked. I had no idea how you'd react."

"You didn't know how I'd react today, either, but you still brought him down. Why?"

"Because seeing you again and not telling you felt like a lie. I couldn't make that decision for you again. You deserved to know."

He regarded her silently. Bringing the baby down here had taken courage. "Thank you."

Some of the tension eased from her expression. "You're welcome."

"What now?"

"I guess...we need to talk about it. But please understand that I don't expect anything from you. You deserve to know, but you don't have any responsibility, here. You're free to go on with your life as if Josh and I don't exist."

He stared at her. "Are you kidding?"

"Not at all." Her expression gentled. "You didn't choose this, Gage. I don't want to saddle you with a child you never intended to create."

"You didn't choose this either."

"Not initially, but after I made my decision, I never looked back. I haven't regretted it for one second. You had no say, though. Expecting you to adjust your life to fit a choice I made is unfair."

He met her gaze. "I don't know what's fair or unfair. This is all so..."

"You're still in shock."

"Yeah." He scrubbed a hand through his hair. "That about sums it up. I need some...time."

She nodded.

"But I can tell you one thing."

"What's that?"

"I could never go on with my life as if you and Josh didn't exist."

2

Ever since yesterday, Emma had spent every waking minute worrying about how Gage would react to this news. She'd only known the fun-loving side of him, which made predicting his response to something life-changing nearly impossible. So far he'd handled the situation admirably.

"This may sound crazy." He glanced over at Josh. "But he looks at me like he knows we're connected somehow."

"That's a sweet thought, but he dishes out that soulful stare to lots of people. My mom, my brother, strangers in the grocery store—they all get that treatment."

"Oh."

"He was giving the lady at the bakery his best melt-your-heart look and she was falling for it. He's a charmer." Much like his father.

She still hadn't adjusted to interacting with him again. Much as she tried to lock down her reaction, he still made her heart race.

He'd had that effect on her every time he'd sauntered into the neighborhood bar where she'd worked. He'd flash her a smile and she'd turn into a puddle of lust.

They'd flirted for a while, long enough for him to learn she wasn't in a relationship. He'd asked her out the first part of December. Both of them were only looking for a fun time with no strings attached.

He'd come into town from the ranch where he'd been working as a wrangler, spend the night with her, and return to the ranch in the pre-dawn hours. Then he'd taken a new job in Idaho and that had been the end of it.

"I should have asked you this before. Are you driving home today?"

His question interrupted her trip down memory lane. "Tomorrow."

"Do you have a place to stay?"

She was *so* glad she'd made arrangements in advance. "The Nesting Place."

He frowned. "I don't—"

"The B&B outside of town."

"Guess I have heard of it. Forgot what it was called." He hesitated. "Do you have to get back to Great Falls right away?"

"I only planned for one night." She kept an eye on Josh, who'd abandoned the coffee table and was crawling across the hardwood floor in the general direction of Gage's chair. "Josh is on the move."

"I see him. Listen, if you could change your plans, I'd like you to stay longer."

"That really wouldn't be conven—"

"I'd pay for it. But we're coming up on a weekend. You might have trouble getting someone to cover for you."

"I'm not a bartender anymore."

Josh stopped halfway across the room and sat down to look around and blow bubbles.

Gage gave him an amused glance before turning back to her. "You left the bar?"

"A month before Josh was born. I started an internet business that I can do from home."

His eyebrows lifted. "What sort of business?"

"I'm a virtual assistant."

"That's cool."

"It's working out great." She was proud of herself for creating a baby-friendly solution for her new life.

"Any chance you brought a laptop with you?"

"I did, but I didn't pack enough clothes or baby food for more than one night."

"I can help you solve those issues. If you're willing to stay." He resumed watching Josh, who'd started toward him again.

"I don't know." She sighed. "Wouldn't it be better if we took a break and let the dust settle?"

"I'm not convinced that's the best way to—well, hello, buddy."

"Da-da!" Josh used Gage's pant leg to pull himself upright. Then he patted Gage's knee. "Da-da-da-da."

"Should I pick him up?"

"Not unless you want to. He's fine right there. It's not like he's asking to be picked up."

"How do you know?"

"He'll try to climb in your lap if he wants to cuddle."

"And are you absolutely sure he isn't saying *daddy*?"

"Positive. It's just an easy syllable for him. He likes hearing himself make noise."

"It's just that he seems so focused when he says it."

Josh chose that moment to blow a raspberry, which always made her laugh. "Great timing, kiddo." She glanced at Gage. The raspberry had coaxed a smile out of him, too.

Ah, that smile. Sunshine through the clouds. She'd put the poor guy through it today. If he needed her to stick around a little longer, then she would.

"All right," she said. "If you can help me find what I need, I'll stay through the weekend and go back Monday morning."

"Great. Thank you."

Josh grabbed onto Gage's jeans and climbed onto one booted foot.

"*Now* he's asking you to pick him up."

"Uh...okay." Leaning over he slid his hands under Josh's armpits and lifted him into his lap. "What do I—oh, hey, there."

Turning in Gage's grip, Josh yawned and snuggled against him.

Gage's reaction was priceless. Shocked surprise was followed by a quick grin that morphed into a relaxed smile of happiness. Then Josh shoved one foot against the fly of his daddy's jeans. Ouch.

Gage winced and gently adjusted the position of that little foot. Then he gazed at her. "Now what?"

"He needs a nap."

"Here? I mean, that's fine, but I—"

"No, not here. I'll head back to the B&B. He'll be better off in the crib they provided."

"Good plan." He looked relieved. "But can I take you both to dinner after his nap?"

"Have you ever eaten in a restaurant with a little kid?"

"Can't say that I have. Why?"

"It might be somewhat different from what you're used to."

"That's fine. I'm flexible."

Dollars to donuts he was clueless. "Wherever we go needs to have highchairs."

"The Eagles Nest Diner should. They cater to families. The food's good. While we eat, we can work out some of the—"

"Don't expect to have an uninterrupted conversation."

"Why not?"

"Usually when I take him out to eat, I spend a fair amount of time monitoring him so he doesn't disturb other people." She marveled at how relaxed he looked curled in Gage's lap. He was fighting sleep, but his eyes kept drifting shut.

"I can help monitor him."

"I also try to minimize fallout."

He frowned. "Fallout?"

"If I don't watch him, he'll get food everywhere, which is okay if he's at home. I spread out a drop cloth, but—"

"Now that you say that, I think we did the same thing with my little sister."

"You have a sister?"

"Yes, ma'am."

She stared at him. "You know what? I just realized that the only thing I ever heard about your family is that they live in Spokane."

"Except they don't anymore. Everyone's moved here. The guy I was sitting with at the bakery is my brother Wes."

"There's definitely a family resemblance." But she'd only had eyes for Gage. Whenever he was around, everyone else faded into the woodwork.

"They're part of the reason I'd like you to stay. They'll want to meet you and Josh."

"Of course." Getting tangled up with his family would complicate things, though. She'd counted on his relatives being conveniently tucked away in Spokane. "Could we wait until tomorrow?"

"We can."

"How many people are we talking about?"

He gazed at her. "My immediate family is only five total—my dad, my sister and two brothers, Wes and Pete. But now there's...you know what? We don't have to go into all of that yet."

"Probably better to wait until we're closer to the time I'll be meeting them. I might not remember what you've told me. I'm a little stressed."

"Join the club."

"Josh sure isn't, though. He's almost asleep."

"Is he?" Gage peered down at him. "Huh. Guess so."

"He must find you calming." Her son was way more chill about this adventure than she was. She didn't find Gage the least bit calming. She took a breath. "Listen, I appreciate the offer of dinner, but I can just pick up some fast food and I have stuff for Josh in the room."

"What's billed as fast food in Eagles Nest isn't fast. You can burn a quarter of a tank of gas sitting in the drive-through waiting for it."

"That's okay. I can—"

"Please let me take you to the diner. If you'll only be here a short time, I want to make the most of it."

She hesitated.

"Think of it this way. You'll have a chance to put me through my paces, see how I stand up under pressure."

"I already did that." She smiled. "You handle pressure just fine."

"That's what you think." His dark eyes sparkled. "You can't see the sweat marks on the back of my shirt."

"Seriously, you did great."

"So did you. Driving down here must have been a scary proposition, but you acted cool as a frozen daiquiri."

"It's an illusion I created by wearing this light green top."

"Which looks nice on you, by the way. Matches your eyes."

"Thanks." The compliment created a flutter in her stomach.

"Your hair's shorter."

"Easier to take care of." With Josh asleep on Gage's lap, the mood was growing more intimate by the second.

His warm glance lingered on her mouth before returning to meet her gaze. "I've missed you, Emma."

Her lips tingled. He kissed better than any man she'd ever been with. But he wouldn't be kissing her now, even if he looked as if he wanted to. "I...I should get Josh back to the B&B."

"Right." He took a deep breath. "Right."

<u>3</u>

Since Josh had fallen asleep in Gage's lap, it was only logical that he should take the little guy down to Emma's SUV. When he stood, the baby melted right into him, boneless and trusting.

The kid was so limp he was afraid if he let go with either hand the kid would slide right to the floor. "Emma, could you please put my hat on for me?"

"I can do that." She picked it up. "Lean down a little."

He stooped so she could reach him. Her scent enveloped him as she moved in close.

"I don't recognize this hat."

"It's my every-day one." He breathed in heaven as she settled it on his head.

"Do you still have the black one?"

"I wore it yesterday."

"Oh. Maybe you did. I was so freaked out I didn't notice your hat."

Ha. That effort had been totally wasted.

She stepped back and glanced at him. "Hang on. The brim needs to come down a little." She made the adjustment. "There. That's better."

"Appreciate it. I would hate to go out in public when my hat's not right." But he was tickled that she remembered how he liked to wear it.

"That's what I figured. I'll go first so I can get the door and unlock the car."

"All right." He took the stairs much slower than she did. Tripping wasn't an option. By the time he reached the gray SUV, she had all four doors open, probably to air it out.

If she lived in Eagles Nest and adopted the habit of the locals, she wouldn't have to do that. On warm days, everyone left the windows down on their parked vehicles. It was just that safe in this small town.

She shoved her sunglasses to the top of her head and gestured to the car seat in the back. "You should be able to slide him in without waking him up."

"Is the seat supposed to be bassackwards?"

"Yep. Much safer."

"But he has no view."

"Which is one reason I don't take him on long trips. This is the most time he's ever spent in a car. Luckily he slept most of the way."

"What happens when he's awake, staring at the upholstery?"

"I sing to him."

"Lullabies?"

"No. He prefers classic country."

Gage smiled. "He got that from me." Maneuvering around the car door, he leaned down and tucked the sleeping baby into the padded seat.

"I'll let you cinch him in. I'm not familiar with these contraptions."

But he'd educate himself because he didn't like the idea that he might not be qualified in this area. Men who'd been given notice of impending fatherhood had time to prepare. He wasn't used to being at a disadvantage in any scenario.

He watched Emma strap the kid in and memorized each step. Got it.

Emma closed the car door and turned to him. "I just happened to think. Is this development interfering with your plans?"

"I'll have to cancel my weekend in Malibu, if that's what you're asking." He stuck his thumbs in his belt loops. "But they love me there and I can reschedule."

"Be serious. Am I taking you away from your job?"

"I'm between jobs."

She frowned. "That doesn't sound good."

"As a matter of fact, it's very good. This is the first honest-to-God vacation I've had since I left home."

"How long have you been out of—I mean, *on vacation*?"

"Since the middle of July."

She stared at him. "But this is September! Is that why you're in Eagles Nest with your family? You can't get work and you're broke?"

"I'm not broke. On the contrary, so don't go telling Josh that his daddy's a deadbeat. I've been saving and I've learned a little something about investing. I can afford this vacation."

"Oh."

"I can also afford to contribute to Josh's upkeep, and that's another thing I know for sure. I plan to do that."

"You're full of surprises, Gage."

"It's my mission in life." But come to think of it, Emma was no slacker in that department, either, showing up the way she had today. "What time should I fetch you and Josh?"

"I'll just meet you there."

Not his style. "I'd rather—"

"The car seat won't fit in your truck. Which reminds me, why isn't it parked out here?"

He shrugged. "The weather was decent. I walked."

"You live near here?"

"Not too far. Anyway, the diner's on Main Street. It's the only restaurant besides the Guzzling Grizzly. Easy to find."

"I'm sure it is. Main Street isn't very long." She glanced up at him. "I can't imagine what it's like living here. This town is really small."

"It's nice, though."

"You like it, then?"

"I do."

"But you haven't found a job, yet."

"Haven't looked."

"Aren't you bored?"

"I was tending in that direction and then a woman I used to date showed up with my kid. I'm not the least bit bored, now."

"Glad I could help." She put on her sunglasses. "You're just as crazy as ever, Gage."

He tipped his hat. "Thank you, ma'am."

"Guess I'd better shove off." She closed the two doors on the passenger side and walked around to the driver's door.

He followed. "Thank you for bringing him down, Emma. I know you didn't have to do it."

She gazed at him. "I think I did. See you at six."

"See you then." He touched the brim of his hat in farewell before returning to the sidewalk.

When she fired up the engine and backed out, he turned away and went back to lock the door. Wes's truck was gone, which meant he'd be hoofing it back to his dad's after all.

He pulled out his phone and read his brother's text. *Had a client call. Hope everything went well. Sorry I can't give you a ride. Leave the key with Ingrid.*

Both Abigail and Ingrid were busy with customers so he waited for a break in the action before walking over to the coffee counter.

Ingrid's brow puckered. "Are you okay?"

"A little shell-shocked. Did Wes give you the deets?"

"A few. We didn't have much time to talk."

Abigail came over, her usual cheerful expression subdued. "How did it go?"

"As well as could be expected." He gave them a quick rundown.

Abigail glanced at the clock on the wall. "Just FYI, this place was buzzing after you left with her and the baby. And news travels fast."

"Meaning someone might have already alerted my dad."

"Maybe not," Ingrid said. "If he hasn't called you yet."

"He wouldn't call. Even if he'd heard something, he'd wait for me to contact him. I'd better text and see if he's home. Excuse me a minute." He sent a quick message to his dad. The instant response—*I'm here*—was all the info he needed. He looked up from the phone. "He knows."

Abigail nodded. "Thought he might. Want a brownie for the road?"

"No, thanks." He dug in his pocket, pulled out the key and handed it to Ingrid. "I put the brownies in Wes's fridge. Emma didn't think giving one to Josh was a great idea."

"Probably not." Ingrid took the key.

"She seems like a good mom," Abigail said. "And Josh is adorable. He has your eyes."

"Yes, ma'am. That he does." He tipped his hat to them. "See you two later." He vacated the premises quickly. After texting his dad that he was on foot and would take a little longer than usual getting home, he set off at a brisk pace.

He'd gone about a quarter of a mile past the edge of town when somebody beeped at him from behind. He looked back just as Kendra McGavin pulled the Wild Creek Ranch van over to the shoulder in the far lane.

She leaned out the window. "Want a lift, cowboy?"

"Yes, ma'am. That would be great." After checking for traffic, he jogged across the road, walked around the front of the van and climbed in on the passenger side. "Were you in town this afternoon?"

"Only drove through on my way home. I went to Bozeman today for—it doesn't matter what I went there for." Her blue gaze was gentle. "Your dad called me."

"Then you've heard."

"Yes. He asked me to watch for you on the road."

"That was thoughtful of him."

"I'll bet this was quite a shock."

"Yes, ma'am. I had no idea."

"That goes without saying. A Sawyer doesn't dodge his responsibilities."

"That's for sure."

"I imagine you two will have a lot to say to each other, so I'm just going to drop you off so you can talk without me hanging around."

"But Dad might want you to be there."

"He always wants me to be there, which I treasure. But you two have a lot of history I haven't been a part of. It's better if I let you have some privacy."

"Maybe so." Her willingness to back off impressed him. He was still slightly in awe of her and a bit wary. He'd arrived on the scene after her romance with his dad had blossomed, while his siblings had been on site to watch it develop.

He was thrilled for his dad, who seemed happier than he'd been in a long, long time. His enthusiasm for this second chance at love was fun to watch.

On the other hand, what was Kendra's role, exactly? She hadn't married his dad and it didn't sound as if she intended to. They lived across the road from each other, not in the same house. She wasn't officially a stepmother.

And yet, she and his dad often functioned as a team, whether with her kids or his. Like today, when his dad had shared the news with her and then asked if she'd give his son a ride on her way home. But she wasn't going to stay and be part of the discussion, and while he liked her a whole lot, he was mostly relieved about that.

He looked over at her. "I don't know if you and my dad had made plans, but I'll be leaving to meet Emma and Josh a little before six."

"As a matter of fact, we don't have plans. I'm getting together with the Whine and Cheese Club tonight. We're going to the diner."

Which was how his luck was running today. "Then I guess I'll see you there."

"That's where you're going?"

"Yes, ma'am. Is this a girls' night out?"

"It is, but we have a purpose. We need to plan Faith and Cody's baby shower and the Guzzling Grizzly has a band tonight. It's too noisy, so the diner was our choice."

"Makes sense." He was invited to that shower for her son and daughter-in-law. He and Pete would be the only unattached guys there. That was still true, but his take on the whole baby situation had done a one-eighty.

"You can ignore us if you want," Kendra said.

"I'll leave that up to Emma. She's agreed to stay through the weekend, but she asked if she could postpone meeting family members until tomorrow."

"The Whine and Cheese Club isn't exactly family."

"Except for you."

She gave him a startled glance. "You think of me as family?"

"Yes, I do."

She flashed him a smile. "Thank you. That's really nice to hear."

"I just wish there was a better designation than *significant other*. That's so weird. And incomplete. Other what?"

"I don't like it, either. And *girlfriend* makes me sound like I'm eighteen, but *lady friend* isn't an improvement. In any case, do whatever you want about tonight. Like I said, you can ignore us."

"I'll leave it up to Emma."

"Good call. What about the flag football game tomorrow?"

"Oh, geez, I forgot about that. What time again?"

"Two, at the park. Listen, if you can't make it, then—"

"But my team needs me."

She laughed. "Yeah, they do."

"It might be the perfect setting to introduce Emma and Josh to everyone. If she totally vetoes the idea, who should I notify?"

"Me. I'm not sure how I ended up being the chief organizer, but I guess I am. I thought Wes was going to be the head honcho for this, or even Ingrid, but they're so busy."

"And you're not?"

"Ah, it's fun for me. I love how it's catching on, how so many are coming out on Saturdays. Eventually the weather will shut us down, but for now, it's great. Well, here we are, and there's your dad, waiting for you."

"So he is." Quinn Sawyer sat in a rocker on the front porch with nothing in his hands. Not a beer or a sketch pad. That was unusual.

The modest house was surrounded by a piece of property about one-eighth the size of the Lazy S, the ranch in Spokane where Gage and his siblings had been raised. After falling for Kendra like a ton of bricks, his dad had sold the Lazy S and bought this place across the road from Kendra's ranch.

She braked the van. "I'm not getting out. Just go."

"Thanks, Kendra." He unbuckled his seat belt.

Her smile was warm. "Anytime, Gage. Now go."

"Okay." He climbed out and started toward the porch. "Hi, Dad."

"Hi, son." He rose from his chair as Kendra drove away and stood waiting for Gage to come up the steps. Then he opened his arms.

Gage accepted the hug with a lump in his throat. Apparently, even though he was thirty years old and had been on his own for quite a while, he'd needed that hug. Stepping back, he took a deep breath. "Rough day."

"I'll bet. Want anything before we sit?"

"No, thanks. Now's not the time to start drinking."

"I figured." His dad motioned to the rockers.

Gage settled in with a sigh. "How much do you know?"

"Roxanne called to report that you left the bakery with a woman who had a baby with eyes exactly like yours. I guess Michael was tending bar at the GG and heard some folks talking so he contacted her to find out what was going on."

"Then you haven't heard from Wes?"

"Nope."

"He's probably still dealing with his client, then. He was at the bakery when Emma walked in. Offered his apartment so we'd have a private place to talk. Later on he sent me a text that he had to go out on a call."

"Emma's her name?"

"Yes. Emma Green. I dated her nineteen months ago for about two weeks that time I was working at a ranch outside of Great Falls. But this never should have happened. I can't believe it did."

"Which tells me it was meant to be."

Gage looked over at him. "You think?"

"That's my take on it. What's the baby's name?"

"Josh."

His dad nodded. "Has a nice sound to it. How do you feel about Emma?"

Now there was a complicated question. When it came to the mother of his child, he was all jumbled up. "I don't know, Dad. She shut the door in my face yesterday, but today—"

"You saw her yesterday, too?"

"Yes, sir. Guess I'd better fill in the gaps to this story."

"Guess so." His dad settled back in his rocker.

Gage laid out the facts as best he could. His dad was a damned good listener. He hadn't appreciated that enough. He finished the story by mentioning the dinner plan for tonight.

"Kendra's going there with the Whine and Cheese ladies."

"She told me. But you know what? I can't introduce Emma and Josh to them before you meet them. That's not right."

"Sure it is. Don't get hung up on that stuff. They'll be here all weekend. What about the flag football game? Wouldn't that be a—"

"That was my thought. Kendra reminded me about it on the way over here and that might be the perfect venue."

"I think so, too. I'll meet Emma and my grandson then."

Gage blinked. "Holy crap." He gazed at his father. "You're Grandpa Quinn."

"Yes. Yes, I am." He smiled. "You're not the only one who got a jolt today, son."

4

Emma changed into a turquoise blouse before driving to the diner. She'd tried to convince herself it had nothing to do with looking nice for Gage and making him proud to be seen with her. But it had everything to do with that.

Josh had left drool marks on the light green one she'd worn today. Although she'd appeared in public with drool marks more times than she could count, she hadn't been escorted by the father of her child in the small town where his entire family lived.

Showing up with a baby in her arms this afternoon and asking for him must have stirred up gossip that he'd have to deal with. She hadn't factored that in because she'd never lived in a small town.

In hindsight, her plan had been deeply flawed. Thanks to her actions, she was caught in a goldfish bowl with limited resources for continuing to look good.

But she'd do her best for Gage's sake. She'd used the bathroom sink to wash out the blouse she'd worn today. Good thing she'd had a total of three, plus another pair of jeans and extra underwear.

That still might not be enough. Life with Josh involved changing clothes a lot. Cotton t-shirts were far less practical than tops made with quick-dry fabrics. Jeans could take a hit whereas skirts could not.

When she was at home in Great Falls, she couldn't care less that her son limited her wardrobe choices. He was a source of joy. And such a good baby. All her friends said so. She hadn't informed any of them about this trip for fear they'd be successful in talking her out of it. But she was glad she'd come.

Life had been simpler before Gage had shown up at her door. But her nagging sense of guilt had hung on like a low-grade fever. Now that was gone.

She found the diner with no problem and pulled in next to his truck. He was still in the cab so he'd likely been waiting for her. He climbed out and met her as she got out of her car.

"You're right on time." He'd changed clothes, too. He wore a snazzy black Western shirt with silver trim and his black hat.

"I figured you'd be waiting." He smelled delicious, damn him. Evidently he still used the brand of cologne he'd worn when they'd dated and he'd applied it recently.

"Listen, before we go in, I need to warn you the Whine and Cheese Club will be in there having dinner."

"Did you say *wine* or *whine*?"

"*Whine.* It's five ladies around my dad's age who've been friends for years and they all know me. I met them at a fundraiser at the Guzzling Grizzly in July. They were dressed in bird costumes."

"How come?"

"Because—never mind. I'll explain later. The important part is that one of them is Kendra McGavin, my dad's...sweetheart. I saw her this afternoon and she told me they'd be here planning a baby shower. She said we could just ignore them if you'd rather not make contact tonight."

"That seems silly."

"I agree."

"Except is it okay if Josh and I meet your dad's sweetheart and her girlfriends before we meet him?"

"I asked that and he said he'll wait until tomorrow. Didn't want to put you under too much pressure."

"Your dad sounds like a great guy."

"The best."

"Excuse me if this is indelicate, but...what about your mom? Is she..."

"She died when I was a kid."

"Oh, dear. I'm sorry." And now she had the urge to hug him, which was not a good idea.

"It was a long time ago."

That might be true, and he'd spoken without much emotion, but his eyes told a different story. Pain didn't have a timetable.

He glanced toward her SUV. "Should we spring Josh? He must be getting antsy just staring at the upholstery."

"Probably, although he'd let us know if he was tired of his car seat." She hadn't forgotten her son, exactly, but his father was a powerful distraction. There was so much she didn't know. She turned and walked around the back of the car.

Gage followed, bringing his spicy, toe-curling scent right along with him. "How about letting me take a stab at getting that little guy loose?"

"Okay." She opened the back door and moved away to give him room.

"I'm curious as to why you put him on the opposite side from you instead of behind you."

"Better line of sight. Easier to keep track of how he's doing."

"Ah. That's logical." He took off his hat and handed it to her. "Would you please hold this?"

"Sure." The luxurious nap of the felt rocketed her back nineteen months. He'd worn this hat whenever he'd stopped by the bar.

Later he'd confessed that he'd done it to impress her. Evidently that had been his intent yesterday, too.

She'd always been impressed by more than the hat, but she'd been charmed by his habit of wearing it every time he came to see her. After she'd finished her shift, he'd follow her home and they'd make love. One time he asked her to put on his hat before she climbed aboard...

"And he's free at last!" Gage lifted Josh from the car seat.

The baby let out a squeal of pleasure.

"Nice outfit." Gage surveyed the miniature Green Bay Packers jersey before hoisting Josh up against his shoulder.

"From my folks. They assume he'll be a Packers fan."

"Like you. I seem to remember you have a jersey just like this."

"Yep. Josh and I were both decked out while we watched the first game of the season on TV." And why bother to mention it? Evidently she was flattered that he'd remembered she owned a jersey that matched her son's. "Want your hat back?"

"Okay." He held Josh securely with one arm while he took the hat in his free hand and settled it on his head.

She envied his ability to balance Josh using only one arm. Now that her son was twenty-six pounds, she required both. Not that she was complaining.

They made a picture, though—handsome cowboy dad and adorable baby. Should she ask them to pose while she got out her phone? No. That could signal a level of commitment she hadn't made. This weekend was very much an experiment.

Josh gazed up at Gage's hat with great interest. Then he stretched his arm toward it and clutched at thin air with his fingers.

"Want the hat, buddy?"

"Gage, you'd better not—"

"No worries. He can hold it."

She was flabbergasted. One of the first things she'd learned after moving here from

Wisconsin was that a cowboy's hat was sacred. Dress hats were guarded with extra care, but even battered straw hats were treated with respect. This Stetson was important to Gage and had likely cost him a fair bit, too.

He took it off and held it by the crown so Josh could get a grip on the brim. "This is a very special hat, buddy. If I hadn't worn it whenever I walked into that bar, your mom would never have given me the time of day."

"That's not true." She'd contradicted him before she could stop herself.

He glanced at her. "If there was more to my appeal, I'd surely appreciate hearing about it."

"I'm sure you would, but—Gage, he's chewing on your hat."

He looked down at Josh, who was gnawing away at the brim of his valuable Stetson. "Well, so he is."

"Don't let him. I don't want him to think that's okay."

"If you say so. Sorry, buddy, but your mom says that's not acceptable." He gently pried his hat away and put it back on his head.

Josh protested and strained upward, trying to reach it.

"My bad, kiddo. I shouldn't have let you have it. Hey look! There's a hawk flying over us." He hoisted Josh up higher. "Wow, that's a big bird."

"Ba-ba!"

"Bird! Did you hear that, Emma? He said *bird.*"

"Well, almost." Gage's enthusiasm was hard to resist. "But I'm afraid he did a number on your best hat. I can see the spot where he chewed on it."

"It's also now my favorite hat." He looked at her, his dark eyes glowing with happiness. "It has my son's teeth marks on it."

"Now that's the way to melt a mother's heart."

"Good to know."

They both laughed, but then his gaze met hers and held.

Oh, Lordy, there was fire in those dark eyes of his. No telling how long she might have stood there soaking up that lovely heat if she hadn't accidentally pressed the panic button on her key fob.

She quickly shut off the alarm. "We should go in. I'll just grab his baby backpack." She reached down and picked it up from the floor of the back seat.

"Isn't he a little small for a—"

"It's mine. I keep all his stuff in it." She hooked the strap over her shoulder and closed the car door.

"That's a great idea." He started toward the restaurant, and despite carrying Josh, he managed to open the door for her.

"Thanks." She walked into a space filled with cheerful voices and the aroma of some of her favorite foods—pot roast, fried chicken, baked potatoes, homemade rolls and coffee. Her mouth watered.

The hostess led them to a small corner booth, left them menus and went to get a highchair. At the far corner of the L-shaped seating area, five women gathered in a large circular booth. Had to be the Whine and Cheese Club.

Gage tipped his hat in their direction before glancing at her. "How about we go over after we order?"

"Works for me."

"I hope you're hungry because the servings are huge."

"I didn't think I was hungry until I walked in and smelled the food. Do you come here a lot?"

"At least two or three times a week for breakfast, but not so much for dinner." He thanked the hostess when she arrived with the chair. Then he tried unsuccessfully to get Josh to put his feet in the opening between the tray and the chair. "Is there a trick to this?"

"He doesn't understand he has to hold his legs straight. You'll have to lift the tray, set him down, and put the tray over his head."

"Got it." He followed her directions and soon Josh was happily slapping his hands on the high chair tray and blowing raspberries.

She grinned at him. "You're a silly boy, Josh."

He giggled and did it some more.

"Did you teach him that?"

"Didn't have to. He learned it all on his own." She unzipped the backpack, took out a container of Cheerios and sprinkled some on the tray before sliding into the booth.

Gage took the opposite side of the booth and laid his hat beside him on the seat. Then he peered at Josh's tray. "Is that his dinner?"

"More like food and a game rolled into one. He has fun picking them up and putting them in his mouth so he's occupied for a while. I brought jars of baby food, too." She looked over the menu. "I smelled pot roast when I walked in. Is it good here?"

"I'm sure it is. I've discovered that Eagles Nesters demand excellence in their restaurants. They only have two sit-down establishments, plus the Burger Barn that features slow fast food. I can testify they're all top-notch."

"Did you just call the residents Eagles Nesters?"

"Uh-huh." He consulted his menu. "I think it's a new term, but it fits. This area's chock-a-block full of eagles, bald and golden, but mostly golden. Other birds, too. Big, little, you name it. Since I'm a fan of birds, I'm happy about that."

"You like birds?"

He glanced up from his menu. "Always have. Why?"

"Josh likes them, too. He'd get all excited whenever he saw one, so I put a feeder in the back yard near a window so he can watch them. He loves it."

"No kidding?"

"No kidding. Word about the feeder has spread in the bird community, too. We draw a crowd, especially in the summer. In fact, I need to text my neighbor and see if she'll take care of filling it over the weekend. Excuse me a minute." She pulled out her phone and quickly typed her request. "Done."

"I wonder if he got that from me." He watched Josh pick up Cheerios one at a time and examine them before popping them in his mouth. "Hey, buddy, are you turning into a bird watcher like your old man?"

Josh paused, a Cheerio held firmly between this thumb and forefinger, and stared at Gage as if contemplating the question. "Da-da!"

"That's me." Gage patted his chest. "Daddy. Dad-*dy*."

Josh chortled and banged his hand on the tray, sending Cheerios flying. "Da-da!"

"Whoa." Gage looked over at her. "Didn't see that coming."

"I'll get my side if you'll get yours."

The server hurried over, order pad in hand. "You don't have to do that. We'll get it later. It's just Cheerios."

Emma straightened and dumped some into her napkin. "I hate to leave a mess."

"Not a problem." The slim, gray-haired woman beamed at her. "Your baby is adorable. What's his name?"

"Josh," she and Gage said together.

"Well, Josh," the server said. "You're a handsome boy."

He gave her his trademark gaze, as if he'd just found the love of his life.

"Oh, my goodness." She smiled. "He's flirting with me."

"He does that," Emma said. "I'll have my hands full in a few years."

"That's for sure." The server glanced at Gage. "I'll bet he learned it from his daddy."

Gage nodded, looking proud. "It's genetic."

Emma ducked her head and swallowed her laughter. It might be, for all she knew. She hadn't met his family.

She ordered the pot roast, a side salad and coffee. Gage ended up with the same. In the short time they'd been together nineteen months ago, they hadn't shared many meals. In addition to the other gaps in her knowledge, she wasn't up on what he liked to eat. Pot roast, evidently.

After the server left, he looked across the table at her. "Ready to meet the Whine and Cheese Club?"

"Sure." She was nervous about interacting with his dad and siblings, but showing off her son to a table full of women? Oh, yeah. She'd relish that experience. So would Josh, the little flirt.

"How much do you want me to tell them?"

Oh. The explanation could turn out to be complicated. Or simple. "How about if you just say this is your son Josh and I'm his mother, Emma?"

"That's it?"

"Do you really want to get into the nitty-gritty?"

He hesitated. "I suppose not."

"Then for now, let's leave it at that."

5

Gage would play it the way Emma wanted. He had the urge to hang a sign around Josh's neck that said *My daddy didn't know!* But that would be pointing the finger at Emma, which wasn't right, either. She had good reasons for not telling him.

Emma was fine with having him carry Josh over to the Whine and Cheese Club table for the introductions. Now that holding the baby was more natural to him, he was eager to show off his son. As they approached, conversation in the booth ceased.

Kendra, who was sitting on one end of the curved seat, was the first to break the ice. "Whatcha got there, Gage?"

"Ladies, this is my son, Josh, and his mother, Emma Green. They're visiting from Great Falls." Emma hadn't told him he could say that but it sounded good, as if he might have been in touch with them all along, maybe even invited them down here. "Emma, that's Kendra there on the end."

"Pleased to meet you, Kendra."

She smiled back. "It's a pleasure to meet you, too."

"Hi, Emma," said the elegant woman with short gray hair sitting next to Kendra. "I'm Jo. What a cute little boy you have."

"Thank you. I'm partial, but I think so, too."

"And next to Jo is Christine." Gage was getting into this. "For the fundraiser I told you about, she was a bald eagle."

"And proud of it. Those costumes are something. Kendra was a golden eagle and Jo was a falcon. Very authentic. We looked like giant versions of the real thing. Might've been too scary for a little one like Josh, though."

"Maybe not," Emma said. "He doesn't scare easily."

"I'm Judy," said the brunette on Christine's left. "I was a pygmy owl because I'm short."

"And I made a great barn owl because I'm so well endowed," said the redhead sitting next to Judy. "I'm Deidre, by the way. Did Gage tell you that we danced to *Shake Ya Tailfeather*?"

She laughed. "No, he didn't. I hope somebody was taking a video."

"There are probably several floating around," Deidre said. "I'll ask who..." She trailed off and looked at the baby. "Hey, Josh, honey, did we know each other in another life? 'Cause I would totally believe it the way you're looking at me."

Josh stared at her in adoration. "Da-da."

She gasped. "He said my name! He said *Deidre*! Or something really close. Freaky."

Gage started to tell her that *da-da* was Josh's default setting and that he was constantly mesmerizing people with his soulful gaze. But why burst her bubble?

"Cheryl just delivered your salads," Kendra said. "We don't want to keep you from your dinner, but thanks so much for coming over."

"Yes, thank you." Deidre said. "We were prepared to let you eat in peace even if it killed us."

"Might as well admit it was mostly killing you, Deidre." Kendra's eyes gleamed with mischief.

"All right, I'll be happy to admit it. Not all of us have the inside track like some people." Turning to Josh, she pressed her forefinger to her ear and her little finger to her mouth before mouthing *call me.*

He bounced in Gage's arms and waved his hands in the air. "Da-da!"

Deidre sighed happily. "I'm in love."

"Oh, boy." Kendra made shooing motions. "Get back to your table, guys. See you tomorrow at the park?"

"I haven't told Emma about that, yet," Gage said. "But like I said, I'll let you know one way or the other."

"Excellent. Hope to see you there."

Emma glanced at him as they made their way back to the table. "What's happening tomorrow?"

"Flag football at the park on the edge of town tomorrow afternoon. I'm supposed to be playing, but I'll cancel out if you—"

"Will your family be there?"

"Yes, ma'am. The whole fam-damn-ly will be playing—my dad, both brothers and my sister, plus me." He tucked Josh back in his high chair.

"How about the Whine and Cheese ladies?"

"They wouldn't miss it."

"Sounds like fun. I'd like to go."

"Then we will." He levered himself into the booth. "But I don't have to play. I'll sit this one out so I can help you with Josh."

"No, you should play." She rummaged in the backpack and came up with a Green Bay Packers bib she tied around the baby's neck. "I have a feeling I'll have plenty of help."

"We'll see how it goes." If she was putting a bib on Josh, then chances were good she wasn't going to eat her salad now, so he'd wait, too. "People are always switching in and out of the game. You could probably play if you wanted to."

"Yeah?" She dived into the backpack again and brought out a spoon and a jar of something that was a disgusting shade of green. "I could play?"

"Why not? You know football and you're in shape."

She paused long enough to glance at him, eyebrows lifted. "How do you know I'm in shape?"

"Nineteen months ago you were and I recognize those jeans so you still fit into them."

Pink tinged her cheeks as she took the lid off the jar. "I don't believe you recognize my jeans."

"Why wouldn't I? I'm the guy who took them off half the time." Yikes, he hadn't meant to say *that*. "Sorry, that was inappropriate."

"Mm." She stuck the spoon in whatever godawful mess she was planning to feed Josh and stirred it like crazy. Her whole face was rosy.

He, on the other hand, was warming up in a different place lower down. Inconvenient. He hadn't the foggiest idea whether he wanted to get physical with Emma again.

Well...not true. He wanted to, but it might be a mistake. And that was assuming she wanted to, which she might not. They had to factor in the effect of their actions on Josh. It wasn't a simple equation of lust equals sex anymore.

"Okay, sweetie," she crooned to the baby. "Time for dinner. Nummy, nummy!" She aimed a spoonful of the green glop at his mouth.

Josh clamped his lips together.

"Come on, sweetie. Open up for mommy. You love this, remember?"

"What is it?"

"Pureed veggies, mostly green beans and peas. I added some asparagus to this batch. He ate it fine two days ago."

"Maybe he was in the mood for it then."

"Well, I'd like him to be in the mood for it *now*." She made another approach with the spoon. "Open wide, baby boy. Great stuff, here. You're gonna love it."

Josh doubled down, his mouth firmly shut as he turned his head away.

"Want to just give him some more Cheerios while we eat?"

"If he fills up on those, then he *really* won't want to eat this, and he needs to. He's a very healthy baby and I want to keep it that way."

"Could I try?"

"Have you ever fed a baby before?"

"No, but I've seen it done in the movies."

That seemed to amuse her. She handed him the jar with the spoon sticking in it. "Go for it."

"You have to make it into a game." He spooned up some green goo. Too bad it wasn't more appetizing. He wouldn't eat this, either. "Here we go, buddy. It's a fighter jet, dodging enemy fire. Pow! Pow, pow, pow!" He zoomed the spoon around and Josh began to giggle.

"That's it! Have fun with it! Here comes the jet. Eat the jet!" He approached the goal, the baby's mouth, open and laughing. Almost there...almost...

Bam! Josh knocked the spoon away and Gage was coated with green glop. One spoonful sure could cover a lot of territory. He had it on his face and down the front of his shirt.

Squealing with delight, Josh slapped the tray and bounced in his seat.

Gage gazed at Emma. She was trying so hard not to laugh that her eyes were watering. He sighed. "Go ahead. It's okay."

She dissolved into giggles that weren't so different from Josh's. And he'd asked for it, thinking he'd learned how to feed a baby from a scene in a movie, a scripted movie that likely had required at least fifty takes before the jet plane strategy had worked.

"I'm sorry." She grabbed a napkin and dabbed at her eyes. "I shouldn't laugh, but..."

"Yeah, you should." He licked his lips where some of the mess had landed. "It doesn't taste as bad as it looks."

"I know. I ate some to make sure it was good."

Picking up a napkin, he wiped the goo from his face. "Do I have it in my hair?"

She grinned at him. "Yes. But if it's any consolation, I've had it in my hair, too."

"I'll bet you weren't in the middle of a crowded restaurant at the time." Damn, she looked pretty when she was having fun. So what if it was at his expense?

"No, I was at home."

He scrubbed his hair with the napkin. "Is it gone, now?"

"It's gone, but your hair looks like you styled it with an electric mixer. And your shirt...your shirt is a disaster."

"It's black. I can just wipe off the—"

"No, don't. You'll rub it in. I sautéed the veggies in olive oil before I put them in the blender. You need to put liquid dish soap on the stains or they're liable to become permanent."

"I'll do that when I get home."

"The longer it sits, the worse it gets. I have an idea. Let's ask them to box up our food and we'll take it to the B&B. Josh eats better when he's not distracted. And I can work on the stains on your shirt."

He didn't have a better plan and the current one wasn't working out worth beans. "Sure, why not?" He caught the attention of their server.

Their meal must have been almost ready, because within five minutes he was in possession of their boxed and bagged dinner. While he paid the bill, Emma carried Josh out to her SUV.

She had him loaded and the motor running by the time he left the diner. She rolled down her window. "Just follow me."

"Will do." He set the bags of food on the floor of the passenger seat so nothing would spill. The rich scent of pot roast filled the cab as he backed out of his spot and pulled up behind her while she waited for traffic to clear.

Didn't take long. In no time, he was cruising down Main, following Emma out of town. The retro street lamps wouldn't turn on for another hour or so, but the businesses closed at six. Some, like Pie in the Sky, locked up earlier. Anyone who wanted to shop in the evening had to drive to Bozeman or Billings.

At first, he'd chafed at that. He was used to having a big-box retailer nearby in case he needed something. Now he liked not having that option. It made for a more relaxed atmosphere.

Or it had been relaxed until recently. His grip on the wheel was a little tight and he loosened it. Then he wiggled his jaw to ease the tension collecting there. Rolled his shoulders to get rid of a crick in his neck. Last of all he blew out a breath. Yeah, nothing was gonna work.

Well, one thing would, but that was a non-starter. He might never have sex again. Look what could happen!

Ever since Emma had walked into the bakery this afternoon, he'd expected to wake up from this crazy dream of discovering he was a father. How could such a thing be real? He was always so careful.

But evidence was piling up that he wasn't dreaming. Nothing about this episode made sense, though. It wasn't logical. His dad had insisted Fate was involved.

Whether it was Fate or a faulty condom, he had a son. That little boy carried his DNA. And Emma's. They hadn't planned to be linked for the rest of their lives, but they were. *The rest of their lives.*

The enormity of it made him slightly sick to his stomach. He'd been so cautious about avoiding long-term commitments. Now he was staring down the barrel of the most binding commitment of all—parenthood. God help him.

6

Ever since Emma had left Green Bay against her parents' wishes, she'd vowed to make it on her own. Having Josh had increased her expenses, but also her determination to meet those expenses. Her online business provided just enough to do that because she was careful about money.

And resources. The dinner Gage had so generously offered would not go to waste and his attempt to feed Josh wouldn't result in a ruined shirt. If he was anything like her brother, he'd throw it in the washer and the dryer without treating those stains.

After parking in the B&B's lot designated for guests, she got out and waved Gage over to a smaller area for visitors. Then she hurried around to the far side of her car to fetch Josh and her baby backpack.

The aroma of pot roast signaled Gage's approach. She slipped on the backpack and hauled a cooing Josh out of his car seat.

"He sounds happy."

She looked over at Gage in the warm light of the setting sun. Damn but he was beautiful, even with food stains down the front of his black and silver Western shirt. "He's a happy baby."

"Probably because of you."

"What a nice thing to say."

"I'm sure it's true. When I met you, I thought you were cheerful because you had to be nice to the customers. But that's just who you are."

"I never saw the percentage in being grumpy." She closed the car door with her hip. "Let's go in. I can smell the pot roast and I'm starving."

"I've been breathing it in the whole way over here. If it tastes as good as it smells, we're in for a treat." He followed her up the walkway to the graceful Victorian. "This is nice. Somebody put money into it."

"Mrs. Stanislowski. I didn't have much time to talk to her, but I did find out she bought it after her husband passed away. He was quite a bit older and left her with enough to open this place. She loves it."

"I can tell. Pots of flowers everywhere and the white trim looks as if someone just painted it."

"It's a lovely place. I was worried when I couldn't find a hotel in Eagles Nest, but this is better." She'd had the presence of mind to shove the front door key into her jeans pocket when she'd left here. Stepping up on the porch, she dug out the key and opened the carved oak door with its etched oval glass insert.

The softly lit reception area was decorated with a harvest theme. Although the autumn leaves and pumpkins were artificial, they looked real, especially with the pots of yellow and orange chrysanthemums tucked into the foliage.

Gage looked around. "Where's the lady of the house?"

"In her private quarters, I suspect. She serves everyone wine and munchies for Happy Hour but that's over. I'm on the first floor. Right down this little hall."

"Smart. No stairs."

"I was lucky she had this one available." As she started toward it, Josh grabbed a handful of her hair and pulled. "Ouch, Josh." She reached up to untangle him but he'd decided it was a game. The minute she got one strand free he grabbed another one. "Josh, stop. That hurts."

"Stand still." Gage put down the bags of food, moved closer and set about prying those little fingers loose. "Hey, buddy, when you go after your mom's hair, you don't mess around, do you?"

"I shouldn't have left it loose. I know better."

"It looks pretty when it's down, though." As he concentrated on the task, his warm breath caressed her cheek and the scent of his aftershave prompted a spike in her pulse rate.

Maybe conversation would dilute the effect of having him so close. "But I should hold off on leaving it loose until he gets over his fascination with it."

He murmured something under his breath that sounded like *I never did.*

"What did you say?"

"Nothing important."

Oh, it might be very important, but she wouldn't press him to tell her.

"You're free." He stepped back. "Maybe I'd better carry him so he doesn't do it again."

"Good idea. I'll take the food."

"Come with me, sport." He scooped Josh out of her arms, which involved more bodily contact.

She took a quick breath before gathering the bags he'd left on the floor and hurrying down the hallway, key in hand. Behind her, Josh giggled, evidently having a grand old time being transported by his dad.

Shifting the bags to one hand, she unlocked the door and went in. "If you'll keep him amused for a few minutes, I'll set us up at the table."

"I think it's the other way around." He closed the door. "He's keeping me amused."

She glanced back in time to see Josh blow a raspberry at Gage. He blew one back. Then Josh made a grab for his hat.

"Oh, no, you don't." Gage took it off and looked around.

"Want me to take it?"

"No, thanks. I've got this." He sent it sailing toward the four-poster that dominated the right half of the room. The hat spun around on the nearest post and came to rest.

"Impressive stunt."

"Thank you. It's been awhile since I've tried that."

Josh crowed with delight and bounced in his arms.

"He wants you to do it again."

"Well, I'm not gonna." He flashed her a grin. "Next time I might miss."

"I sincerely doubt it." Smiling, she carried the bags and her backpack over to a small table. It sat by a window with a view of a sweet little garden that was still visible in the fading light. An antique high chair sat by the table along with two chairs.

While Josh and Gage traded laughter and raspberries, Emma turned on the light in the kitchenette and set the table with the dishes in the cupboard. She got out Josh's food and sliced up a banana for his desert. Then she started a pot of coffee.

"I always liked that song."

She looked up, startled. "What song?"

"The one you were humming just now." He dodged Josh's attempt to grab his nose. "*Could I Have This Dance?*"

"I didn't even realize what I was doing." Her cheeks grew warm. Evidently the cozy domestic scene had prompted her to start humming. "Ready to eat?"

"You know it." He brought Josh over to the high chair. "Whoa. Different configuration."

"Let me slide the tray back. Mrs. Stanislowski bought an antique one to match the décor."

"I like it." He deposited Josh in the chair and she locked the tray back into place. "What kind do you have at home?"

"One something like this. I'm a sucker for vintage."

"I guess I am, too. This place is great. I'm glad you suggested coming back here to eat."

"Oh! One of the reasons was your shirt. I forgot about that. If you'll take it off, I'll start it soaking while we eat."

"Ah, never mind the shirt. It'll be fine."

"The stain is getting more embedded by the minute and that's a gorgeous shirt. I'll feel terrible if Josh has ruined it. Your hat is bad enough."

He smiled. "Then I'll have a shirt that reminds me of him, too."

"Don't be silly. Take it off. I insist."

"Alrighty, then." He unsnapped the cuffs and pulled the bottom loose from his jeans. Then he worked his way down the front, revealing bare skin. No white t-shirt.

Uh-oh.

He paused. "Is something wrong?"

"No, no. I just thought...don't you usually wear a t-shirt?"

"In the winter, but not in the—oh, I get it. When you pictured me taking off my shirt, you expected I'd still have a t-shirt on underneath." He began refastening the snaps. "Let's not worry about this right now."

"But I—"

Josh banged on his tray and squealed.

"He's hungry." Gage glanced at him. "We'd better—"

"I'll feed him in a minute. I want to work on that stain. It's not like I've never seen your naked chest."

He gazed at her. "But that was different."

She didn't dare get lost in that gaze. Sure as the world she'd see her own hot memories reflected there. "I'm saving that shirt, whether you want me to or not. Take it off."

"You sound determined."

"I am."

Josh squealed again.

"Then let's do this." Snaps popped as Gage pulled the shirt apart and took it off. "Here you go. Where's Josh's jar of goo?"

She cast a quick glance over Gage's muscled chest with its sexy dusting of dark hair. As seductive as ever. "On the table with a spoon, but you don't have to feed him."

"Might as well try. It's not like he's going to mess up my shirt."

"Guess not." She took the shirt to the kitchenette, ran some water over the stains, and pulled a bottle of dish soap from under the sink.

While she squirted it on the back side of the stain and rubbed it in, she took several deep breaths. She could do this. She could eat a meal with a shirtless Gage Sawyer without ogling him.

Leaving the shirt to soak, she turned around.

Heaven help her. Sharing a meal with a shirtless Gage might have been doable. But he'd just upped the ante.

Jar in one hand, spoon in the other, he was feeding Josh. No fighter jet games, no elaborate tricks. Instead he softly coaxed her son to accept one spoonful after another.

Somehow, in the short time Josh and his father had been together, they'd bonded. For Gage to be casually feeding his son wearing nothing but his jeans and boots was the most natural thing in the world. And beautiful.

7

Gage looked over at Emma. "I have no idea why he's being so cooperative."

"That's easy. You nailed the hat toss."

He grinned. "Yeah, I'm sure that's it. Gets 'em every time." Returning his attention to Josh, he scooped up another spoonful and the little guy opened his mouth. Feeding him was a thrill and a half.

The green stuff was nasty to look at but as he'd discovered when some had hit him in the face, it tasted decent. This baby food was the first thing he'd eaten that Emma had cooked. He'd spent his nights with her but had driven back to the ranch at dawn every morning. He'd never stayed for breakfast.

The jar was almost empty. "Go ahead and start eating." He spooned in some more green stuff. "We'll be done in a minute."

"I'll wait. I'll pour our coffee, though. You want some, right?"

"Yes, please. Does Josh get something to drink?"

"I'll give him his sippy cup after he eats the banana."

"He's done with bottles?"

"I didn't do the bottle routine. I nursed him until recently, and he went from that to his sippy cup."

His son had done a lot of growing up that he hadn't been around to see. He'd missed Josh's first smile, his first laugh, his first tooth. "When's his birthday?"

"September twenty-first."

"A week from today." He didn't want to miss that, too.

"It's coming up fast."

"Have you made plans?"

"Not really. My parents are both teachers so the timing is bad for them to come out here at the beginning of the school year. They wanted me to fly back there with him and at first I was going to. But I changed my mind."

"How come?" He scraped the last of the green glop from the jar and popped it into Josh's mouth.

"I'm not sure it would make sense to anyone else."

"Try me."

"Montana is my home, now. Josh is a Montana kid. I don't want him to spend his first birthday in Wisconsin."

"Sounds about right to me." He handed her the empty jar. "How about coming down here? My family would love to celebrate his birthday."

"But they haven't even met him, yet." She carried the jar over to the sink.

"Doesn't matter. My family's all about birthdays." Something else he hadn't appreciated enough. "Josh is the first grandchild. I can guarantee they'd be thrilled if they could throw him a party."

"I'd still like you to check with them."

"I'll ask tomorrow. What's the plan for the banana?"

"Just a few pieces at once."

"Okay." He plucked five slices out of the bowl she'd put on the table and laid them on the tray of the high chair. "What would happen if I dumped the entire bowl on his tray?"

"He'll mash it into oblivion."

He laughed. "The kid in me wants to see that happen."

"Have you ever tried to clean sticky bits of banana off a floor?"

"Can't say I have."

"Then curb your impulse to give him all of it at once. He won't be able to resist driving his fist into a mound of banana slices."

"Come to think of it, I might not be able to resist, either. Some things are just meant to be squished."

She took a seat at the table. "I've never had that thought in my entire life."

"Which supports my theory that girls are different from boys."

"They *are*?" Her eyes widened in mock disbelief.

"Yes, ma'am. And I, for one, am very happy about that." He began spooning his dinner onto his plate.

"So am I." Her gaze rested for a moment on his bare chest, then skittered away.

If having him sit there without a shirt bothered her, oh, well. He'd tried to talk her out of it. Exactly *how* it bothered her interested him a great deal, though.

If he had to guess, he'd say the chemistry was still very much there, but she was conflicted about it. That put them in the same boat. And the stakes were way higher now. Josh was involved.

They couldn't afford to do anything that might cause problems in what was now a complicated relationship. Easier said than done when Emma had insisted that he strip down.

Taking off his shirt was a trigger because that had been one of the first things to go whenever they'd made love. Being bare-chested clearly affected her, but it affected him, too.

The gesture had awakened his instincts and energized his body. Removing his shirt in front of Emma had always meant that something was about to happen, something exceedingly pleasurable.

Not tonight, though. He dug into his meal because at least that was one hunger he could satisfy. For a while, silence reigned as they ate their dinner and Josh was busy with his banana slices. Gage kept him supplied, adding more when the tray was empty. No smashing went on.

"That's it for the banana," he said when Josh picked up the last slice and crammed it in his mouth.

"I'll get his sippy cup." She went into the little kitchen area and came back with it, along with a washcloth. "Time to clean you up, sweetie-pie."

Josh scrunched up his face and flailed with his hands as she wiped away excess banana, but he cooed with excitement when she finally gave him the sippy cup.

"Wow, he handles that like a pro."

"He has excellent coordination for his age." She took the washcloth back to the kitchen and returned to the table.

"Of course he does. He's my—I mean *our* son."

She laughed as she sat down. "You can take credit for his good coordination if you want. I doubt I could have landed that hat on the bedpost."

"You could if you'd practiced as much as I have."

"Oh, really? On whose bedpost?" She picked up her fork and started eating the last of her dinner.

Did he detect a slight tinge of jealousy in that question? "I don't need one to practice. I grew up on a ranch. Posts galore. This was my first actual bedpost."

"I see." She looked happy about that. "I didn't realize Josh and I were witnessing such a momentous event."

"Oh, yeah. One for the record books." He picked up his coffee mug.

"Was this ranch where you grew up in Spokane?"

"Outside of it. The Lazy S. My dad sold it in May." He took a sip of his coffee.

"Then he hasn't been in Eagles Nest that long, either."

"No. Everything happened pretty fast, which is why it caught me off guard. I'd never felt untethered before, but I sure did once I couldn't go back to the Lazy S. Didn't matter that I seldom visited. It was just the idea that it was there if I wanted to."

"I can see why that would be disorienting."

"No kidding. I didn't know the ranch meant that much to me until it was gone. Suddenly I felt the need to quit my job and move here so I could hang out with my family again."

"How's that working out?"

"Great. I'm glad I did it. For one thing, I have a new appreciation for my dad. For years he was the dependable anchor for the rest of us. But he needed the freedom to grow and change, too. Now he has it."

"And what does he think about this new development?"

Gage decided not to bring up the *meant to be* remark. "He's excited to have a grandson, although he's a little freaked out that he's suddenly a grandpa. I don't think he was quite ready for that."

She smiled. "This is the first one, then?"

"Surprisingly, yes. Roxanne's engaged and Wes is moving in that direction, but nobody's produced a kid. Until now."

"Let me guess. You were the least likely candidate."

"No question." He swallowed the last of his coffee. "What about your family? Any other grandkids?"

"No. My brother's not ready to settle down, either."

"Either?"

She blinked. "I did just say that, didn't I? Force of habit. Then again, maybe I don't think of having a baby as settling down. I'm still single. I don't answer to anyone and my only real responsibility is to Josh."

"You like being your own boss, then."

She met his gaze. "Absolutely."

"That makes two of us. I think that's part of the reason we were attracted to each other." Although he'd wanted to ask her out from the moment he'd gazed into her luminous green eyes. He'd been mesmerized. Still was.

"I think you're right. I've always avoided needy men and you've never struck me as that type. Cocky, yes, but not—"

"Cocky?" He pressed a hand to his chest. "You wound me, madam."

"No worries. It just adds to your charm." She said it with a smile in her voice.

She was also looking at him in a way that brought a rush of heat to his groin. In the past, he would have taken that as a sign that she was open to the idea of getting naked.

It couldn't mean that now, of course, but that didn't stop him from reacting. "We had some good times."

"Yes, we did." Her lips parted and her breathing grew shallow.

Oh, hey, now. He wasn't imagining this. He knew exactly what was going through her mind.

The same thing that was going through his. His jeans began to pinch.

Right on cue, Josh banged his sippy cup on the tray of the high chair. "Da-da!"

Gage dragged in a breath. "I should go."

"Your shirt is wet." She sounded breathless.

"Probably a good thing." Getting out of his chair was slightly painful but he managed it. "It'll cool me off." Leaning down, he kissed the top of Josh's head. "Later, big guy."

Grabbing the shirt from the sink, he wrung it out and shrugged into it as best he could. He left it hanging open. "I'll be in touch about tomorrow."

She pushed back from the table. "I'll walk you to the—"

"That's okay." He gave her a quick smile. "I'll see myself out." He propelled himself through the door, down the hall and out into the cool night air. Another second in that room and he would have hauled her out of her chair and kissed her, baby or no baby. And she would have let him.

8

Gage called the next morning while Emma was sitting on the floor with Josh. He'd chosen one of his favorite toys, multicolored stacking cups.

Sometimes he stacked them inside each other and other times he'd give her one to hold, periodically exchanging it for a different one. But mostly he banged them together and chortled in glee at all the noise he could make.

Her stomach fluttered as she answered the call. "Good morning."

"Hi."

One syllable in his deep baritone and warmth flooded her body. She took a breath. "What's up?"

"I have info, but I hear a bunch of noise in the background. Is this a bad time?"

"It's perfect. Josh is busy playing."

"Okay, then. First off, I asked my dad about the birthday celebration. You should have seen his face. He just lit up."

"Aw, that's sweet. Would your sister and brothers like to be part of it, do you think?" She gave Josh the blue cup and took the yellow one he offered.

"Um, yes. And that's the tip of the iceberg. My dad called Kendra, and—"

"Oh, right. She should be there."

"She has five sons."

"Teenagers? That could be fun."

Josh took the yellow cup and give her a green one while murmuring *da-da* under his breath.

"Kendra's boys are all around my age."

"They are?" She exchanged another cup with Josh. "She doesn't look old enough."

"She had them very young. Two are married and the others are in relationships. What I'm trying to say is that this party is going to be—"

"Huge?" She gave Josh the cup she was holding and he used it to bang against another one and chant *da-da* in a singsong voice.

"Yes. What's going on there, anyway?"

"Josh is practicing his act in hopes someone will launch a *Toddlers Have Talent* reality show."

Gage chuckled. "Then be sure and get a video."

"I have videos. Way too many videos."

"From when he was younger?"

"I do."

"Then maybe I could see them sometime."

"Definitely." Her chest tightened with guilt. Had she made a terrible mistake, not contacting him sooner? Nothing to be done about it, now, but his wistful tone as he'd asked about videos would haunt her.

"Anyway, the b-day party is turning into an extravaganza, but I hope you still want to, because they're all super excited about it."

"It sounds terrific, Gage. Thank you."

"Believe me, once I said *my son's first birthday* it was like throwing a whole bag of tortilla chips out to the birds. Everybody's in. You might want to put together a list of gift suggestions. Lots of people want to know what to buy him."

"Heavens, I don't expect people to bring presents."

"I guarantee they'll all want to and if you don't give them ideas, no telling what you'll end up with. Not everybody in this group is savvy about babies, including me. And I want to get him something."

"Okay. I'll give it some thought." Yesterday she'd arrived in Eagles Nest expecting that Gage would be the only person involved in this drama. Judging from the event he was describing, half the town wanted to celebrate Josh's birthday.

"Anyway, that's that. Since flag football's at two and we'll both need lunch beforehand, I was thinking I'd make some sandwiches and come by around noon, if that works for you."

"It does and I appreciate it. I have Josh taken care of, but I hadn't figured out what I'd do about eating."

"I'm the one who asked you to stay, so let me worry about that. Which reminds me. I can take you shopping after the game. Whatever you need—food for Josh, extra clothes, diapers—we can pick it up today."

"That would be helpful."

"One last thing. Kendra wondered if you'd be willing to come to the ranch for dinner tonight. She has a high chair and other baby stuff. She said it would just be you, me, Josh, my dad and her."

"That's a lovely gesture. Do you want to go?"

"I want to do what makes sense to you."

"Well, if I'm reading this situation right, Kendra is taking on the role of Josh's grandma."

"I'm pretty sure she is. With enthusiasm."

"Then I can't imagine denying Josh the experience of having her as a grandma."

"I can't, either. What do you want on your sandwich?"

"Whatever you have. I'm not picky."

"Then it looks like it'll be P, B and J."

"Okay."

He laughed. "I can do better than that. How does turkey, cheese, lettuce and tomato sound?"

"Delicious."

"Mayo? Mustard?"

"Mustard."

"Yep, me, too. See you at noon."

"See you then." She disconnected and looked at Josh. "Hey, my little friend. I think you're about to become a local celebrity."

Giggling, he bounced and used his stacking cups like cymbals.

"Oh, you'll be a hit without even trying very hard. The big question is how I'll go over with this crowd since I kept you a secret for so long. Can I ride on your coattails?"

Josh gave her his heart-melting gaze. "Da-da."

"Right. His coattails, too."

The rest of her morning zipped by. She checked email and responded to several clients, fed Josh an early lunch, gave him a bath and put him in his crib with some toys so she could take a quick shower.

Gone were the days when she could experiment with makeup and try on several outfits before she chose one. She wore her second pair of jeans and the only top that Gage hadn't seen yet. Splashed with green and gold, it was more dramatic than the other two.

By some miracle she'd brought gym shoes and she'd put those on in case she had a chance to play. She'd caught her hair up in a ponytail.

The hoop earrings she used to love were tucked away in a jewelry box at home because shiny, dangling things were irresistible to her curious son. Eventually she'd wear them again, but it wasn't worth the potential hazard.

She stuffed the baby backpack with everything she could possibly need at the park. She put sunscreen on her and Josh. She laid his floppy hat on top of the backpack so she'd remember to put it on him. Wearing it ramped up his cuteness factor by at least a thousand percent.

By the time Gage rapped softly on her door at noon on the dot, she was reasonably well-organized. And nervous. Dealing with her folks had been difficult, but at least she'd told them about Josh the day she'd had the pregnancy confirmed.

She'd kept the Sawyer clan out of the loop until now, though. She'd been focused on how the news would affect Gage but hadn't factored in the grandparent and nephew angle. Gage had mentioned how excited they all were, but would anyone be upset because they were just finding out?

Then Gage walked through the door and she lost track of everything but his sexy self in a snug white t-shirt and navy sweats. He had a backpack slung over one broad shoulder. She stared at the transformation from cowboy to jock. "You're wearing a ball cap! And sneakers!"

"Athletic shoes." He grinned. "You can't play flag football in jeans and boots. Doesn't work."

"That lets me out." She glanced down at her jeans. "But I see your point. These don't have enough give to them."

"Kendra anticipated the problem." He lowered the backpack to the floor, unzipped it and pulled out a pair of gray sweats and a white t-shirt. "After meeting you last night she decided you might fit into her clothes."

Touched by the gesture, she smiled as she took them. "Here I've been obsessing over whether anyone would be upset because I waited so long to tell you about Josh. Instead they're offering me clothes so I can play flag football with them."

"That's how it is in Eagles Nest. It took me a while to get used to it, too." He glanced down as

Josh crawled over and grabbed a fistful of his pants leg.

But tugging on the soft material didn't give him the leverage he needed. He plopped down on his bottom and held up his arms. "Da-da!"

"Hey, buddy." Warmth flowed through his voice as he reached down and hoisted Josh into his arms. "Who's your daddy, huh? Who's your daddy-o?"

"Da-da." He patted Gage's cheeks.

"Right on, big guy. Right on." He looked over at Emma and winked. "I'm choosing to believe."

"Go right ahead." She was becoming a believer, herself. "If you'll take charge of him for a minute, I'll duck into the bathroom and change."

"Sure thing. I like that blouse, by the way," he called after her. "Looks great on you."

"Thanks." And now she wouldn't have to worry about it getting messed up playing football. She'd had a hunch her jeans wouldn't work, either, but they were all she had.

After closing the bathroom door, she nudged off her shoes and pulled her blouse over her head. Clacking noises and laughter from both Josh and Gage indicated they were on the floor playing with the stacking cups.

Gage's voice filtered through the door. "Let's try rolling one, okay, buddy? Here it comes. Catch it!"

Josh squealed in delight.

"Sending over the blue one, now. Ready?

"Ba-ba!"

"Right! The blue one! Wait for it. Rolling...rolling...and there you go! Great catch!"

More squeals and baby laughter.

"Hey, Emma, everything okay in there? If that stuff doesn't fit, maybe we can—"

"They're fine! Be right out." And they probably would be fine if she took the time to put them on instead of standing there riveted by the sounds of Gage playing with Josh. Ignoring what was going on beyond the door, she quickly peeled off her jeans and put on the sweats and the women's cut t-shirt. They both fit perfectly—not too tight and not too baggy.

She picked up her clothes and shoes and opened the door just as Gage rolled another cup over to Josh. Her son snatched it up with a cry of triumph.

"Great job!" Gage had turned his hat around rally-cap style, making him look even more like an athlete. He glanced at her and smiled. "Nice."

"Thanks. I guess Kendra's right that we wear about the same size." His casual compliments gave her spirits a boost. Male appreciation had flowed in a steady stream during her bartending days. Although she wasn't hooked on that kind of thing, it was nice when it happened.

But now that she was a mom and worked at home, it didn't happen very often. Coming from Gage made it even nicer. She wasn't ready to examine why that might be. Not yet.

9

After a quick lunch, Gage led the way over to the park. He couldn't wait to get there so everyone could meet Emma and Josh. Yesterday afternoon in the bakery had been awkward as hell, but today would be much better.

No doubt some folks, including members of his family, were speculating what would happen next. He wished them luck guessing that because he didn't have a clue. He was taking it one day at a time.

This afternoon, though, promised to be a wagonload of fun. When he'd heard about the flag football project, he'd been one of the first to sign up. He looked forward to every game, but today Emma and Josh would be there, making it more special.

He parked in line with the other vehicles near the field and Emma pulled her SUV in next to him. Players and spectators mingled along the sidelines as they set up folding chairs and beach umbrellas. Several had brought coolers.

He met Emma by the back door next to Josh's car seat. "Is it okay if I take him out and carry him over there?"

"Sure." She gestured toward the crowd. "So many people! I had no idea."

"It's become a popular spectator event." He opened the car door, took out the baby backpack and set it on the ground. Then he unbuckled the straps holding a cooing, bouncing Josh. "I think somebody's ready to party. He has the hat for it, too."

"He knows when I put on his hat he's going outside, which he loves. He's been babbling the whole way over. Are all these people going to play?"

"Only the ones dressed like we are." He lifted Josh out and tucked him in the crook of his arm while he closed the door and picked up the backpack, slinging it over his other shoulder. "You can tell who's just here to watch because they're wearing boots and jeans."

"I'm seeing a pattern in the way the players are dressed. The shirts are either red or white."

"That's our version of team jerseys. They're the Rowdy Reds and we're the Wacky Whites."

"So I'm on your team?"

"Yes, ma'am. I asked Kendra to assign you to the Whites. Is that okay?"

"It's okay." She grinned at him. "But for all you know, I could be lousy at this."

"We'll take our chances." He glanced at Josh, who had gone silent. The baby's eyes were wide as he looked around. "He's not scared, is he?"

"Nope. He cries when he's scared. He's just taking it in. He's never seen so many people before. His big outing is to the grocery store, and I time those trips for when it's not crazy busy."

"Just so he's not overwhelmed."

"I'll let you know if I think he is. Here, let me take the backpack. You don't have to—"

"Actually, I do if I want to show off my daddy chops."

Her eyebrows arched above her sunglasses. "Your daddy chops?"

"Indulge me, please."

"All right. Thank you." She fell into step beside him as they started toward the field. "Why don't you point out your family members so I can start memorizing names?"

"Good idea." He surveyed the crowd.

"I've already found Kendra, so is the guy next to her your dad?"

"That's him. And see the tall woman with the long black hair standing near Dad?"

"Uh-huh."

"That's my sister Roxanne, and her fiancé Michael Murphy is the guy with his arm around her waist."

"Roxanne and Michael. Got it."

"Wes and his girlfriend Ingrid should look familiar since they were both in the bakery yesterday."

"I do recognize them. Okay, so that's Wes and Ingrid. You have one more brother. Where's he?"

"Pete's the guy talking to Wes."

"Pete's blond?"

"Right. He's the only one of us who inherited my dad's light coloring. I could point out all the McGavins, too, but—"

"I'd better stick with just your family for now."

"Makes sense. But I have a tip for identifying Kendra's five sons."

"Let's hear it."

"Remember how blue her eyes are?"

"Yes, I noticed that. Amazingly blue."

"In Eagles Nest, that color of eyes is called McGavin blue, and her boys inherited it. If you see a guy with eyes like hers, guaranteed he's one of her sons. She has five of them."

"Will they all be here?"

"Maybe not. One's a volunteer firefighter and two others lead trail rides for Kendra, so it all depends on who has time off."

"I'm sure I'll figure out who's who as we play. One other thing. How come some of your family's wearing white and some red? Aren't you all on the same team?"

"A few people thought it would be fun to mix it up. Couples can choose to be on the same team or not." He shifted Josh in his arms. "How're you doing, buddy? Ready to go meet Grandpapa Quinn?"

"Pa-pa!"

Gage stopped in his tracks. "Emma, did you hear that?"

"Yes."

"Has he ever said it before?"

"I don't know. Maybe. Not often. But I don't think—"

"I know. It's not like he knows he's talking about his grandfather. But if he says it to my dad and my dad buys it, let's just let him think Josh knows what he's saying."

She smiled. "Sure, why not?"

He wanted to kiss her for that. Hell, he'd been wanting to kiss her for a dozen reasons. This was just the most recent. "Thank you."

"Anytime."

* * *

They'd been spotted. People quickly looked over their shoulders but were polite enough to turn around again instead of continuing to stare. Emma thanked her lucky stars that she was used to meeting new people and answering questions. Bartending had prepared her for just this kind of scenario.

So had the road trip with her friend Janet, which had opened up possibilities that wouldn't have occurred to her if she'd stayed in Green Bay. When she'd hit Montana, she'd decided this was the place where she'd plant herself and grow.

But she never would have predicted an accidental pregnancy with a dashing cowboy who was only supposed to be a fling, someone to warm a handful of winter nights.

He was good with Josh, though, better than she'd expected. He carried his son with pride as they approached the knot of people waiting beside the large blue cooler and a collection of unoccupied folding chairs. Once someone in the group had seen them, the rest had stood.

Gage made straight for the tall, broad-shouldered man with the awestruck expression in his gray eyes. "Dad, I'd like you to meet Josh. Josh, this is your Grandpapa Quinn."

The little ham belted it right out. "Pa-pa!"

Quinn gasped. "Did he say what I think he did?"

Gage shrugged, playing it cool. "Sounded like it, Dad."

"Will he come to me?"

"Not sure. Let's ask. Josh, want to go see Grandpapa Quinn?" He stepped closer to his dad. "I promise he'll spoil you rotten."

"Will not."

Next to him, Kendra had her phone out. "Don't be ridiculous, Quinn. Of course you will. Look at that little goober."

"What do you say, buddy?" Gage moved a little closer. "Want to make a new friend?"

"Hey, Josh," Quinn said quietly. "Come give Papa a hug. I'll make it worth your while."

"Oh, dear God," Roxanne said. "He's already bribing the kid. Dad, have you no shame?"

Quinn chuckled. "None whatsoever. I want to hold my grandson. Come on over, Josh." He raised his hands to shoulder height and wiggled his fingers. "My family wants a photo op."

Without warning, Josh launched himself in Quinn's direction.

Gage gently transferred the baby to Quinn as phones lifted along the sidelines to record the moment.

Emma cursed her own lack of planning. Her phone was in the backpack Gage had slung over his shoulder. But Kendra was snapping away, so she'd likely share whatever she'd taken.

A photo might not capture what was happening with Quinn, anyway. He'd gathered Josh against his chest. Her son was gazing up at him as if trying to figure out how this new person fit into his life. Then Quinn leaned over to murmur something to Josh that was clearly meant to be private.

Emma strained to hear it, anyway. Sounded like *I'll love you forever, little buddy.* Her throat tightened. If Gage hadn't come to see her, none of this would have happened. But he had, and because of that, her son was in the loving arms of his grandpapa.

<u>10</u>

Emma was still focused on the sweet tableau when Gage laid a hand on her shoulder. "Dad, I'd like you to meet Josh's mother, Emma Green."

Quinn glanced up and smiled. "I'm happy to meet you, Emma Green." Shifting Josh to his left side, he held out his hand. "And grateful." His grip was warm and strong.

"I'm happy to meet you, too, Mr. Sawyer." Judging from the kindness in his eyes, if he hadn't been holding Josh he would have hugged her.

"Just Quinn, ma'am."

"It's a pleasure, Quinn." No wonder Gage thought so highly of his dad. He exuded positive energy.

"And this is my sister Roxanne."

Emma held out her hand. "I'm glad to—"

"I'm thrilled that you came down." Roxanne's dark eyes sparkled as she grasped Emma's hand in both of hers. "And Josh is absolutely adorable."

"Thank you." Roxanne's gaze was familiar, so like her son's...and his daddy's.

Roxanne turned to the broad-shouldered man at her side. "This is my fiancé, Michael, and I think you've already met Wes and Ingrid."

"Not officially, though." Emma shook hands with everyone. "Wes, you were a lifesaver yesterday."

"Glad I could help."

"And last, but not least," Gage said, "there's my big brother Pete."

"Who's also known as *Uncle* Pete, now." He gave her a broad smile. "Pleased to meet you, Emma." His large hand engulfed hers. "I plan to study up, find out what this uncle thing is all about, make sure I get it right."

She laughed. "No worries. I'm sure you'll be great at it."

"Hey, yeah," Wes said. "I'm an uncle, too. I forgot that part."

"Personally, I think Auntie Roxanne has a musical lilt to it." Gage's sister glanced up at her fiancé. "Uncle Michael sounds good, too."

"But should I be Uncle Michael or Uncle Mike?"

"Or Uncle Mikey," Pete said with a grin. "That has a certain ring to it."

"Okay, okay, you uncles, aunties and grandpapas." Wes turned to survey the group. "Now that Emma's been introduced to all the usual suspects, are we ready to play some football?"

"Normally I'd be rarin' to go," Quinn said. "But as I seem to have my hands full, I'm hoping Emma will agree to take my place for a bit."

"I'd love to."

"Excellent. Thank you."

"Here's the baby backpack, Dad." Gage set it down beside him. "In case you need anything."

"You know what?" Kendra gazed at Quinn and Josh. "I think I'll sit out for a while, too. I'll go tell Ryker."

Emma looked at Gage. "Who's Ryker?"

"Her oldest son. He's team captain and center for the Rowdy Reds. Big guy, ex-military."

"Who's our team captain? Oh, wait, I'll bet it's Wes since he's handing out the flag belts." She moved into a lunge position to stretch her leg muscles.

"Well, now." Gage folded his arms. "Something tells me you've done this before."

She gave him a quick smile as she continued with her stretching routine. "Some."

"Am I about to be really glad I asked for you to be on the team?"

"We'll see, won't we?" She strapped on the belt Wes handed her. "Let's go play some football." Energized by the prospect, she jogged out to the field.

The game turned out to be even more fun than she'd anticipated. She stole flags left and right, carried the ball several times and scored once. Being out there with Gage and working in tandem with him on some of the plays was a blast.

Eventually she managed to ID three McGavin brothers—Ryker, Cody and Zane. About the time she needed water and a break, Wes brought subs in for both Gage and her.

Breathing hard, Gage headed for the blue cooler, opened it and handed her a water bottle.

Then he took one for himself. "Great job out there."

"You, too." She gulped some water. "That last spiral you threw was a beauty."

"Thanks. You have good hands. I should have guessed you'd be excellent at this." He wiped his face with the hem of his t-shirt, exposing his taut abs.

Oh, baby. She allowed herself one quick ogle before glancing away. "My brother taught me all I know."

"Oh, yeah? I don't think you ever mentioned his name."

"It's Connor."

"Does he live in Wisconsin?"

"No, he's off doing his thing down in Texas. He's even picking up an accent. It's very cute." She finished off her water. "Speaking of cute, we need to check on Josh and your folks. They might be ready to play, now."

"I don't know about that." He laughed as they walked toward the group of chairs. "They look mighty happy holding court with Prince Josh as the star attraction."

"And Josh is soaking up the attention." Currently Kendra had him in her lap while Deidre, also wearing a red shirt, was making faces at him. The rest of the Whine and Cheese Club had gathered, too. A woman she hadn't met who looked to be six or seven months pregnant sat next to Quinn.

"Hey," Quinn called out as they approached. "You two covered yourselves with glory. I have a hunch Emma's played this game a time or two."

"I have, and football's my favorite sport to watch."

"She's a Packers fan," Gage said. "She's from Green Bay."

"Well, have a seat, Packers fan." He stood and waved her into his chair.

"I don't need to take your—"

"No, no, I insist. Faith has been hoping to talk to you about baby stuff. Have you two met?"

"We have now." Emma sat down and held out her hand. "Emma Green."

"Faith McGavin." She had a no-nonsense handshake.

"She's Cody's wife," Quinn said.

"Cody! That guy's one heck of a football player. He got my flag twice."

"Yeah, he loves these games." Faith tossed her blond braid over her shoulder. "I played, too, until running wasn't so much fun anymore."

"I can imagine."

"Okay, Grandpapa Quinn," Kendra said. "I'm handing Josh over to Deidre so you and I can go play some football."

"Hallelujah! Come to Auntie Deidre, my little cutie patootie."

"Da-da!"

Emma rolled her eyes. "It should be interesting next week when he doesn't have his crowd of adoring fans."

"He sure is social, though," Faith said. "I hope I end up with one like that."

"What's your due date?"

"December seventeenth," Faith said. "And I can't wait."

"Are you having a boy or girl?"

"We want that to be a surprise. We'll be happy with either, but I'm pretty sure Kendra's hoping for a girl after raising five boys."

"I get that, although she's been awesome with Josh."

"Good point. She'll fall in love with our little whozit no matter which we have. Our family is large and boisterous, though, so I'd love for our baby to be as easygoing as Josh. Is that something you've worked on?"

"He's always been good-natured, but I've also established a routine and I think that helps. This weekend's not so structured, but at home he's on a regular schedule."

Faith nodded. "That probably helps prepare him for something like this, where everybody wants to get acquainted with the little squirt."

"Includin' me." A muscular guy in a red shirt approached the group. "Greetings, ladies, Gage. Miss Emma, Badger Calhoun at your service." He sketched a quick bow.

She glanced up at him. "Nice to meet you, Badger. I'll bet you hail from south of the Mason-Dixon line."

"I'm a Georgia boy, ma'am. I can see by your perplexed expression you're wonderin' how I fit into this crowd."

"Actually, I was wondering how you got the name Badger."

"Explainin' that would take longer than a Southern preacher's sermon, so it'll have to wait for another time. But I sure would love to meet this little bundle of joy y'all made."

"I've got possession, Badger, sweetie," Deidre said. "You can hunker down and say hello, but you'll have to wait your turn if you want to hold him."

"Badger!" Ryker shouted from the field. "You're in for Pete!"

"Aye, aye, Cowboy!" He glanced at Josh. "Catch you later, little dude. My team captain calls." He trotted onto the field.

Pete arrived, breathing hard, water bottle in hand.

Gage left his chair and clapped a hand on Pete's shoulder. "You okay, bro? Saw you take a tumble a few plays ago, but I didn't think—"

"That was nothing." Pete grinned and shoved his fingers through his sweat-darkened blond hair. "Noticed Badger poaching the nephew I have yet to hold." He took a swig of water. "Asked Ryker to switch us."

Deidre sighed. "I suppose you have dibs, then, Pete. But please give him back when you're done."

"I can do that, ma'am." He put down the bottle and wiped his hand on his shirt before holding out his arms. "How about it, big guy? Want to soak up some honest sweat from your Uncle Pete?"

"Pa-pa!"

"Whoops, got some confusion going on there," Deidre said. "Here you go, Uncle Pa-pa."

"Deidre!" Ryker's commanding voice rang out. "You're in for Roxanne!"

Deidre stood with another resigned sigh. "Guess I should have seen that coming. Auntie Roxanne doesn't want to be left out." She gave Josh a quick kiss on the cheek. "Don't have too much fun without me, snookums."

Roxanne arrived, snatched up a water bottle and handed Deidre her flag belt. "Thanks for going in for me."

"I get it, Auntie Roxanne. I was just warming him up for you two." She hurried toward the field.

Roxanne put down her water bottle and smiled at Pete. "A nice brother shares with his sister."

"But I just got him."

"Okay. Timed possession." She looked at her sports watch. "You get ten minutes and I get ten minutes."

"Deal."

A whistle blew. "Halftime!" Wes called out and the entire field of players started in their direction.

Emma got up and stood beside Gage. "I wonder if anyone's coming this way hoping to hold Josh."

"If so, they're out of luck." He seemed amused as he watched Pete making faces at Josh and Roxanne consulting her watch. "You don't mess with timed possession."

"Sawyer family tradition?"

"Yeah." He laughed. "I'd forgotten about it. Mom taught us that. Usually put an end to our arguments."

"Great idea."

"She had a lot of them." His smile faded. With a quick swallow, he glanced away.

11

Normally, Gage had very few flashbacks about his mom. He was having more now because he was hanging out with Josh. That much was obvious. But after all these years, they shouldn't pack such an emotional punch.

He didn't like it, especially because Emma's concerned expression told him she'd noticed. Time to change the subject. "Will you be ready to go back in when the break's over?"

She took a moment to answer, as if she was onto his avoidance maneuver. Luckily she didn't press the issue. "I'm ready to go back in, but Josh is due for a nap."

"How do you want to handle that?"

"I managed to cram one of his thin blankets and his favorite stuffed animal into the backpack. I'd like to find a spot where we can put him down on the grass for a little while during the second half."

"I know just the place."

"Great. Let's go tell Roxanne that we'll take him when her time is up."

"Follow me." Taking her hand, he worked his way through the crowd until he stood next to

Roxanne. "Hey, sis. When your time's up, we need to take that little guy. Emma thinks we'd better put him down for a nap."

"With all this commotion? How would that work?"

"We have a plan."

"Oh. Did you hear that, Josh? They have a plan to get you to take a nappy-poo." She leaned forward and rubbed noses with him, which made him giggle. "I *hated* naps. I'd pretend to be asleep, but as soon as they left me alone, I'd get up and play."

"Don't go giving him ideas, sis."

"But that's what aunties do, big brother."

"Did I hear that somebody's going down for a nap?" Ryker walked toward them.

"If he doesn't, he's liable to get cranky," Emma said.

"This sweet little darlin'?" Badger came over and joined them. "The one who's always smilin'? Your mama doesn't know what she's talkin' 'bout, does she, Josh?"

"Ma-ma." He reached out both hands toward her.

"Aww." Roxanne gave him a kiss. "If you want your mommy, then over you go." She passed him to Emma.

Gage glanced at her. "How about asking my dad and Kendra if they'll watch him for a bit after we get him settled? Then we could play some more."

"That would be great, if they want to."

"I'll bet they will." With Emma by his side, he headed toward his dad and Kendra. As he'd predicted, they were delighted with the plan.

Scooping up the baby backpack, he led Emma and Josh over to a quiet spot under a maple tree. It was a fair distance from the field so the noise would be somewhat muted. The leaves were just starting to turn, with a few bright spots of red in the thick foliage. The grass underneath was still green and soft.

He glanced back at Emma. "How's this?"

"Perfect. If you'll hold him, I'll get out the stuff. I want to give him some water in his sippy cup once we have him on the blanket."

He put down the backpack and took charge of the baby. "You know what, Josh? Your mom's very organized. I'll bet that's one of the reasons you're so calm. You know you can depend on her."

"Thanks for that." Emma shook out the blanket, soft blue with rainbows on it. "Bartending taught me a lot. If you don't plan ahead and make sure you have everything you need, you get unhappy customers. And lousy tips."

"I can't believe you ever got a lousy tip."

"A couple of times, but that was on them, not me. Some people are just cheap." She poured a little water in Josh's sippy cup and snapped on the lid. "You were always generous."

"As I've established, I was trying to impress you."

"Well, it worked." She gave him a quick smile.

"Yeah, but you quit that job. How am I supposed to impress you, now?"

She glanced up. "Do you want to?"

He'd been joking around. She'd gone and tossed that joke back at him, giving it significance he hadn't intended. He knew the answer, though. "Yes, ma'am. I do."

She held his gaze. "Then just keep doing what you're doing."

Oh, boy. He had absolutely no clue what he'd been doing, but if he said so, he'd look like a doofus. After the first shock of discovery, he'd been playing it by ear, going with the flow. He had no plan. Maybe she thought he did and if so, he wouldn't disabuse her of that.

He took a deep breath. "Okay, I will." Whatever that meant.

She smiled, so it must have been the right answer. "Here's what I'm thinking for Operation Nap. You sit him on the blanket and I'll immediately hand him his sippy cup to give him something to do. If we plop down on either side of him, we can grab him if he decides to crawl off. Once he finishes his water, I'll give him his birdie."

"His what?"

"It's a little plush toy, a bluebird of happiness. He loves birds so much I got him this when he was about six months old. It's his favorite and he sleeps with it."

"Huh. That's cool. Okay, let's see what happens." He lowered Josh to the blanket so he was sitting squarely in the middle of it. Emma gave him the sippy cup and he started drinking.

Gage sat on the baby's left. "So far, so good."

Emma eased down on the opposite side. "I have no idea if he'll sleep."

"Well, yeah. The game's kind of loud, but I don't know what we can do about that. Take him back to the car, I guess."

"I'd rather not. It's so nice out here. If we once get him to sleep, noise won't bother him. One time he was taking a nap and a neighbor decided to cut down a tree with a chainsaw. Josh slept right through it."

"Amazing."

"But he's never taken a nap outside, so I don't know if the unfamiliar surroundings will keep him awake. This spring and summer he played outdoors quite a bit, but I've always taken him in when it was nap time."

"Then let's try it and see what happens. If he won't go to sleep, then there's always the car."

"Good strategy."

He watched as dappled sunlight played over Josh's blond hair. And Emma's. All his previous memories of her were nighttime ones. This was nice. "Sitting here reminds me of camping. Do you think Josh would like that?" *Would you?*

"I have no idea, but probably. You're talking about a tent, right?"

"Yes, ma'am."

"Well, he loves it when l make a tent for him in the house with a sheet and a card table."

"I used to love that as a kid, too. Then I bought myself a tent and sleeping bag when I was around twelve. I don't know what happened to it. Dad gave me the box of my stuff that he packed up when the ranch sold, but nothing was said about my camping gear. I'll have to ask."

"I camped as a Girl Scout. Haven't done it since. I remember it being fun, though."

"It is fun." He gazed at her, on the verge of asking if they could go sometime and take Josh. He could always buy new camping equipment. Probably should, anyway. "Maybe we—"

"Da-da!" Josh dropped his cup, got onto his hands and knees and started toward Gage.

"Whoa, buddy." He blocked the baby's progress. "Stay on the blanket, okay?"

"Here's his birdie. Catch." Emma threw it to him.

He snagged it and held it out to Josh. "Look what I found, sport."

"Ba-ba!" Pushing himself back to a sitting position, he reached for the soft little bird. Its plush fur was matted in places, as if he'd been sucking or chewing on it.

"Here you go. Here's your birdie." Gage handed it to him.

The baby's voice dropped to a whisper as he took the bird in both hands. "Ba-ba." Then he held it out to Gage. "Ba-ba!"

"I see it, buddy. That's a really great birdie you have there." He glanced at Emma. "What now?"

"Let's lie down on either side of him. He loves mimicking people's behavior. He might just lie down, too, since he has his birdie." She stretched out on her side in the grass. "Ah, Josh, I'm sooo sleepy. Time to go sleepy-bye, Josh."

"Me, too, sport." Gage settled down and rested his head on his outstretched arm. "Sooo tired. Time to go to sleep."

Josh studied him for several seconds. Then, his birdie clutched against his chest, he rolled to his side. "Ba-ba."

"Sweet dreams, little guy."

Slowly Josh's eyelids drifted down.

Gage waited until he was sure the baby was asleep. Then, as stealthily as he could manage, he propped himself up on his elbow and looked over at Emma.

It took great self-control not to suck in a breath. She was so beautiful lying there in dappled sunlight, her gaze soft and a tender smile on her lips. But he clamped down on his natural response. Nothing he wanted to do right now was appropriate to the circumstances.

Instead he mouthed the words *he's asleep.*

She gave a slight nod.

Be right back.

She nodded again.

He did his best to move quietly as he got to his feet, although the chainsaw story gave him hope they could pull off this nap now that they'd achieved the critical step. He gave Emma a smile before turning and walking toward the sidelines.

His dad and Kendra sat in folding chairs talking with Faith and Roxanne.

Kendra glanced at him. "Did you get him down?"

"Sure did. Emma says once he's out, he can sleep through anything, so monitoring him shouldn't be a big deal."

"I'm not worried about it." She got up. "Come on, Grandpapa Quinn. It's our first babysitting gig."

"Can't wait, Granny Ken."

Gage laughed. "Granny Ken? Where did that come from?"

"It's my grandma name. When Faith and Cody made their big announcement, I decided to choose my own so I wouldn't get saddled with one I didn't like. Now I just need to make it stick."

"And I intend to help her with that project," his dad said.

"Alrighty, then. Do you want to take your chairs?"

His dad smiled at Kendra. "Hey, Granny Ken, do you think these old bones of ours can handle sitting on the grass?"

Kendra stooped a bit and added a quiver to her voice. "Lord-a-mercy, I don't know, Grandpapa Quinn. My lumbago's been acting up something fierce. How about you?"

His dad pitched his voice an octave higher. "I don't rightly know what lumbago is, but if you've got it, I'm sure I've got it, too, my little muffin top."

"Get out of here, you two."

"We'll endeavor to totter over there without falling down, son." His dad winked at him before taking Kendra's hand and ambling over toward the tree.

Once they'd relieved Emma, she came hurrying over. "What's the score?"

"Tied," Roxanne said.

"Gage and Emma!" Wes called out. "You're up!"

Emma flashed him a big ol' grin. "Let's go win this thing."

"Yes, ma'am." Maybe he was impressing her a little, but she was impressing the hell out of him.

She was resourceful, resilient, loyal and gutsy. Nineteen months ago, he'd been fascinated by her beautiful eyes, silky hair, and lithe, responsive body. But he'd barely skimmed the surface. There was so much more to Emma Green.

_12_

Football was in Emma's blood and she hadn't had this much hands-on fun with it since she'd left Wisconsin. The first half she'd concentrated on getting grooved in. But she was there, now, baby.

She threw herself into the action—snatching flags, catching lateral passes, whirling away from defenders. She suggested a play and managed to score another goal, breaking the tie. She was on fire.

But so were the Rowdy Reds. Ryker was a damn good player. He led his team to another goal, tying it up again. Not much time left.

In the huddle, Emma turned to Gage, who was quarterbacking. "Look for me. I'll get open."

"Gotcha."

They lined up and she leaned over, hands on her knees as Gage called the play. Gage took the snap and turned. Defenders swarmed, but he whirled away from them, searching for her.

Ducking into a hole in the defense, she waved her arms.

He spun, looked, and threw her a perfect spiral. Great arm.

She leaped, caught the ball and ran like hell for the end zone. She looked back once and Ryker was charging after her with his teammates racing behind. Too late! Touchdown!

Lifting the ball in the air, she did a little victory dance until her team descended, whooping and smacking her hand with high fives.

Gage raced toward her, lifted her off her feet and twirled her around. "Awesome catch!" Then he gave her a quick hug and backed away, his grin lopsided. "Really awesome."

"Thanks."

When she returned to the line of scrimmage, adrenaline coursed through her body, both from the excitement of the play and the sensation of being twirled around by Gage. She'd missed being held in his strong arms.

The game didn't last much longer and she never got her hands on the ball again because the Reds put their best defenders on her. But she managed to pull one flag, allowing the Whites another possession. The Reds didn't score in the time left.

"You totally won the game for us." Gage was in high spirits as they walked to meet Quinn and Kendra. Quinn carried a sleepy Josh and Kendra had slung the backpack over her shoulder.

Gage relieved her of it. "Did you guys see Emma catch the winning pass?"

"I did," Kendra said. "Grandpapa Quinn was busy with Josh."

"He woke up that quick?" Emma calculated how long he must have slept. Not enough. His head lay on Quinn's shoulder and he clutched his birdie in one little fist.

"He did," Quinn said, "but we had quiet time. He still got some rest, I think."

Kendra smiled. "Grandpapa Quinn entertained Josh with stories about Gage's antics when he was a little boy."

"Telling him all my secrets, huh, Dad?"

Quinn chuckled. "He was a rapt audience."

"Me, too," Kendra said. "I learned so much about you, Gage."

"Don't believe a word of it. My dad has a vivid imagination."

"And total recall," Quinn said.

Emma gazed at this little miracle, a second set of grandparents she'd never expected Josh to have. "I can't thank you enough for watching him while Gage and I played. That was special."

"Special for us, too." Quinn adjusted his hold on Josh. "I'll be happy to carry him to the car."

She didn't doubt it. He was beaming, as if he'd be happy to carry that baby anywhere he needed to go. "Let's do that. He looks very contented right where he is."

As they all started toward the parking area, she and Kendra walked ahead of the guys, who'd launched into a recap of the game.

Kendra glanced over at her. "How soon can you make it to the ranch tonight?"

"Gage mentioned taking me shopping so I can pick up a few things, and I'd like to shower and change. I'd say a couple of hours, if that's okay."

"It's fine. You should get there before dark in case you want to have a look around."

"I'd love that. I haven't spent any time on an actual ranch."

"Do you ride?"

"Not at all, but I'd like to learn."

"Well, you've come to the right place. We're all about horses and riding. Cody and I led a trail ride this morning. Got back just in time for the game." She scanned the parking area. "Where's your vehicle?"

"I'm in the gray SUV next to Gage's truck. On the far side of the lot."

Kendra turned around and walked backwards as she called out to Quinn. "Hey, boys, get a move on, please. Emma needs to go shopping before the market closes."

Emma looked at her in surprise. "Will it close soon?"

"At five on Saturdays." She pivoted and continued toward Emma's SUV. "You can make it, though."

"Five, really?"

"Yep. And closed on Sunday. We're a little retro in Eagles Nest."

"I'm getting that. When I drove down Main last night all the shops were closed except that cute little drugstore."

"Pills and Pop. The owner likes to stay open a little later at night and for a few hours on Sunday, mostly because of the soda fountain."

"There's a soda fountain in there? The old-fashioned kind with a counter and stools?"

"Yep. Plus a couple of booths and a jukebox."

"No way."

"I learned to dance at Pills and Pop. So did all five of my sons. High school kids still hang out there after school."

"That is so cool. I wonder how many of those soda fountains are even left?"

"Not many." Quinn came up behind them. "Better watch out, Emma. Kendra will have you moving to Eagles Nest before you can bat an eye."

"It has a lot of charm, for sure. I can see why she loves it here. I can't remember the last time I ate a hot fudge sundae while sitting on a stool at a soda fountain."

Quinn winked at Gage. "I think that's what they call an opening, son."

"We should go tomorrow," Gage said. "Josh would love it, too."

And Quinn was doing some matchmaking. She smiled. "Yeah, he would."

"Good. That's settled," Kendra said. "We need to get these folks on their way, Grandpapa Quinn."

"Roger that." He started toward the SUV.

"Wait, my keys are in the backpack and I need to unlock it."

"Oh...right." Quinn paused. "Man, I really have acclimated to this place. I've completely ditched that habit."

"Here you go." Gage handed Emma the backpack.

She took it, dug out the keys and pressed the button that unlocked the doors. "Are you saying people don't lock their vehicles in Eagles Nest?" She walked over to her car and opened the back door so Quinn could tuck Josh into his seat.

"Or their doors, in many cases," Kendra said. "Businesses do, and maybe some folks who live in town, but out where I am it's common to leave doors unlocked. We just don't have crime around here."

"That's appealing."

"I'm telling you, she's a walking chamber of commerce." Quinn glanced over his shoulder. "I might need help with this operation. Things have changed since I last used one twenty-five years ago."

Emma opened her mouth to explain the process.

Gage beat her to it. "I'll show you, Dad." He proceeded to give detailed instructions on how to strap Josh into the car seat.

Kendra sidled over to Emma. "Where did he learn that?"

"The man's a quick study."

"Takes after his dad. Quinn's kids are a talented bunch. I've had fun getting to know them."

"I'll bet." Emma was still processing her encounter with the Sawyer family.

Their warm acceptance of both her and Josh was sweet and uncomplicated. Making the effort to maintain that connection through the years was a no-brainer.

Looked like she'd be maintaining a connection with Gage, too, judging by how devoted he'd been to Josh so far. That connection was sweet in many ways, too. And more complicated than any she'd ever faced.

_**13**_

The Eagles Nest Market was about half the size of the grocery stores Gage had been used to before moving here. Because he was fascinated by the design and layout, he'd made a point to meet the owner.

Otto Schlitz was a throwback to the days before superstores and automated checkout lanes. By keeping his operation small, he could oversee every department. He was there every day, all day.

Gage held the door for Emma and Josh. "You're gonna love this place." Then he shut up because he didn't want to oversell it.

She glanced around before turning back to him with a smile. "You're right, I am."

"Thought so. Let's get a cart. Josh will get a kick out of that part."

"He already adores shopping carts, so...oh, my goodness." She stared at the bright red cart Gage wheeled in her direction. "He gets a steering wheel?"

"And even better, he faces forward so he can actually see what's going on instead of being blocked by whoever's pushing the cart."

"Da-da!" Josh bounced in Emma's arms when he got a glimpse of the cart. "Da-da-da-da!"

"Such a treat, Josh!" Emma set him into the molded seat and fastened his seat belt.

Gage laughed as the baby grabbed the steering wheel immediately and started turning it. "I'm so glad you needed to go shopping. I wouldn't have missed this for anything."

"If we lived here, he'd want to go every single day." She grasped the cart's handle and surveyed the store. "Then again, I would, too. It's unique."

If we lived here. She'd said it so casually, as if it might be on the table. Might be best not to twist his brain around that subject right now.

But he was glad she liked the market. "I figured you'd be intrigued. Otto's part grocer, part interior decorator."

"Otto?"

"The owner. In fact, here he comes. Hey, Otto!"

"Gage, you brought your baby to see me! *Wunderbar!*" The portly, silver-haired man hurried over, all smiles. "I heard you're a papa, now. What a handsome boy, too. And dis must be—"

"Emma Green, Josh's mother. Emma, this is Otto Schlitz."

"Pleased to meet you, Mr. Schlitz."

He grasped her hand in both of his. "Call me Otto, beautiful lady. Or call me handsome. Dat's fine, too. Gage, what a lovely woman to be the mama of your baby. And just look at him, little

Josh. He has Emma's hair and your eyes, a perfect blend of you two."

"Thank you." Emma's hand remained enclosed in both of his. "I love the design of your market, Otto."

"Me, too! I combined Old Country wid New World. Old-fashioned wooden shelves, but I painted dem bright colors, like a child's playroom. And I wanted dem lower dan what you see in some stores. Who wants to go into a maze where you can't see out? Look out from my aisles and you can see the whole store!"

"I like that, too, and the produce displayed in woven baskets, and your farm tables with buckets of apples and pears and plums. I love it all."

"Of course you do, pretty lady. You have good taste. You chose dis man to be your baby's daddy."

"Oh!" Her cheeks turned pink. "I—"

"Don't tell me you didn't choose him because I know dat's what ladies do. The men tink dey choose and you let us tink dat. But you, you're looking for a perfect man. And see? You found him!"

Emma was flustered and Gage was no help. Not a single snappy comeback occurred to him. Otto had romance in his soul and contradicting his rosy view of the relationship would only upset him.

"I've kept you here talking long enough." Otto squeezed Emma's hand and released it. "You came in to shop. But let me give dis little boy something before you go. What would he like?"

Emma glanced at Gage in alarm. "He doesn't need any—"

"How about a pretty apple? Josh, do you want one of dese apples? Here, I'll choose two. You tell me which one, okay?" Picking up a rosy Pink Lady and a deeper red Gala, he held them out to Josh. "Which one?"

"Ga!" Josh reached for the Gala.

"Den dis one it is." He handed over the apple. "Wid my compliments. Tell dem at checkout I gave the baby an apple so dey don't charge you for it."

"Thank you, Otto." Gage extended his hand. "I appreciate your generosity to my family." *My family.* He'd never said the words in this context before, but Otto was so convinced they *were* a family that confirming it seemed like the thing to do.

"Yes, thank you, Otto," Emma said. "It's been a pleasure meeting you."

"My pleasure, entirely, sweet lady. Please come back again soon."

"I'd like that."

"And now we really do have to get our shopping done." Gage rested his hand on Emma's shoulder.

"Of course, of course." Otto waved them off.

Gage left his hand on Emma's shoulder until they'd moved a distance away. "Sooo, that's Otto. He's kind of—"

"Old school. I know. Love his accent. But we need to watch Josh. He's liable to drop that apple or pitch it somewhere."

"I'll keep an eye on him."

As it turned out, he didn't have to worry about the apple ending up on the floor or landing in someone else's cart. Josh kept firm possession of it, turning it this way and that, gnawing on the stem and pressing his mouth to the smooth surface.

As Gage tucked him into his car seat after loading the purchases into Emma's SUV, Josh insisted on keeping the apple with him.

Emma shook her head. "An apple. Who knew?"

"Otto."

"Yeah." She laughed. "So this is where we part ways, right? I'll meet you at Wild Creek Ranch around six."

"Do you know how to get there?"

"Not yet, but once I put Wild Creek Ranch, Eagles Nest, Montana, into my phone, I'll know exactly how to get there."

"So true." Seemed like he should kiss her goodbye, especially after listening to Otto rave on. "See you then." *Stop thinking and just do it, idiot!* Sliding an arm around her waist, he pulled her toward him and kissed her. He didn't linger too long, didn't use any tongue.

But her lips felt welcoming, even for that brief time. Their mouths fit together without a lot of shifting and adjusting. That wasn't true of everyone he'd kissed. The rest of them fit together nicely, too, but he'd best not dwell on that.

He let go and gazed at her. "Is that okay?"

"Guess so." But the warmth in her eyes told him it was very okay. That she might even want him to try it again sometime.

He rubbed the back of his neck. "I can't speak for you, but I haven't felt this awkward around a girl since I was in middle school."

"Not me. I've never felt awkward around girls."

He grinned. "Smart aleck."

"See you at six."

"Yes, ma'am." He wouldn't mind kissing her again, but Josh was in the car staring at the upholstery, although at least now he had an apple to hold. "See you at the ranch."

"We'll be there."

He backed away, holding her gaze. Yep, just like middle school. Heaving a sigh, he turned and headed for his truck.

* * *

Gage and his dad drove over to Kendra's together, which put them there early because his dad wanted to help with dinner. Gage was perfectly happy to do that, too. While lasagna baked in the oven, he shucked corn, his dad made the salad and Kendra set the table.

She came back into the kitchen. "Is Emma still nursing? Or can I offer her a glass of wine?"

"She's not and she might like some wine. She is a former bartender, after all."

"Okay, great. What about Josh? Is he eating solids?"

"Banana slices. I don't know about anything else. I'm sure she'll bring his sippy cup with her. And probably a jar of her homemade baby food."

"My boys used to love chewing on an ear of corn at that age. That might be fun." She looked at the kitchen clock. "She should be here any minute but we're pretty much ready. I just need to get the high chair out of Cody's room."

His dad put down the knife and the tomato he'd been about to slice. "I'll do it."

"Ah, but you look so sexy making that salad. Carry on, please."

He grinned at her. "Yes, ma'am."

"I do love a salad-makin' man." She left the kitchen.

"So, Dad." Gage kept his voice down. "Will you two ever get married?"

"I doubt it, but we might have a fun little commitment ceremony. Nothing official...just a great party and a solemn vow."

"Interesting idea. And you'd still live on opposite sides of the road after that?"

"Why not? I'm quite attached to my studio. The light is perfect and the space suits me. Kendra likes having her private time, too. It works for us."

"I heard my name," she called out from the dining room. "Whatcha talking about?" She walked in the kitchen.

"He asked if we're ever getting married. I said no."

"Oh." She turned to Gage. "Would you like us to?"

"It's just that if you did, even if it's only that fun little ceremony Dad was talking about, I could start calling you my stepmom instead of all the other options we talked about yesterday."

"Was that only yesterday? Seems like more time has gone by." She gazed at him. "The thing is, I can't promise when your dad and I will get around to that ceremony."

"Well, right. Everyone's busy."

"How would you feel about calling me your stepmom now instead of waiting until then?"

Warmth filled his chest. "You'd be okay with that?"

"I would be honored."

"Me, too." He swallowed. "Me, too." He walked over and hugged her. "Thanks. I—" The clack of the door knocker kicked his pulse into high gear. "That must be Emma and Josh. I'll get it." He hurried out of the kitchen.

When he opened the massive front door, Emma stood there wearing the pretty green and gold top he'd admired earlier today, the one that complemented her green eyes and golden hair. Otto was so right. She was stunning.

Josh let out a squeal of pure joy. "Da-da!"

"Hey, big guy." He scooped him out of her arms and stood back so she could come in.

"I think he missed you."

"Yeah?" He pushed the door closed and looked at Josh. "Did you miss me, buddy?"

"Da-da." He reached up to pat Gage's cheeks with both hands.

"Smooth, huh? I shaved, just so I could do this." He leaned down and blew a raspberry against the baby's soft neck, which started him giggling.

"Welcome to Wild Creek, Emma." Kendra walked over and gave her a hug. "I'm so glad you could come."

"So am I. What a beautiful place."

"I agree." His dad hugged her, too. "I'm grateful that Kendra lets me hang out here."

"I never expected an actual log ranch house."

"It was here when my folks bought the property," Kendra said. "They told everybody they bought it for the log house."

"I can see why. It's amazing." She took off her backpack. "The sunset was spectacular when I was driving in. The clouds are just right to capture the color. Did you see it?"

"We were all in the kitchen," Gage said.

"I'm sure it's still pretty if you want to go out and look."

"Great idea," his dad said. "I'm always up for a good sunset." He opened the front door and held it while Kendra and Emma walked out. Then he grinned at Josh and tickled him gently on the belly. "Missed you, little buddy."

Josh giggled. "Pa-pa."

"I think he missed you, too, Dad." He met his father's gaze and smiled. "Let's go soak up some sunset."

"I'm right behind you."

"Ohhh, look at that!" Out in the yard, Emma turned in a circle. "I think it's even better than before."

"It's a beauty, all right." Kendra said. "I wanted you to see the place before it got dark, and it looks even better when it's got this pinkish-orange glow. Gorgeous."

And so was Emma. Gage was captivated by the sight of her as she rotated slowly beneath the crimson sky so she wouldn't miss a thing. She clearly loved nature and being out in it.

But how could he have ever discovered that when he was her lover? They'd spent all their time indoors, mostly in her bed. Sure, that had been crazy good, but so limiting.

"Ba-ba!" Josh pointed at the sky.

Gage glanced up as a pair of goldens wheeled above them on the swirling air currents. "Good eye, buddy! Birds! Eagles!"

Kendra looked at Emma. "Does Josh like birds?"

"He really does. That's why he has that little plush bluebird."

"Then he should also like Raptors Rise."

"I can't believe I didn't think of that." Gage turned to Emma. "We should go there, too."

"What is it?"

"It's a rescue facility for birds of prey. Zane—you remember who he is, right?"

She nodded. "From this afternoon. Yes."

"It's his project and he's built it into quite an operation. That's what the fundraiser was for, the one where the Whine and Cheese Club dressed in bird costumes."

"Oh, wow. When do you think we could go?"

"Maybe tomorrow. It's right down the road from here."

"If Zane's available, I'm sure he'd like to give you a private tour," Kendra said. "Let me text him when I get in the house. In fact, I need to check on the lasagna. Gage, why don't you show Emma around the ranch while I finish in the kitchen?"

"I can do that."

"And I'd like to give my grandson a tour of the house," Quinn said. "Let him explore the place before dinner." He glanced at Emma. "Would that be all right?"

"You know, he probably could use the exercise. He's used to roaming my house and the room at the B&B is a lot smaller."

"Good deal." He walked over to Gage and held out his arms. "Come hang out with your grandpapa, Josh. Let's see what kind of trouble we can get into."

Josh bounced with eagerness and stretched out his arms. "Pa-pa!"

Gage passed Josh over to his dad. "He's good at motoring around a coffee table."

"I figured. We'll have us some adventures, won't we, kiddo?"

Josh bounced some more. "Pa-pa-pa-pa!"

"Now say bye-bye to Mommy and Daddy." He picked up the baby's arm and helped him wave. "Bye-bye. Bye-bye."

Josh flapped both arms. "Bye-bye!"

Emma stared at him. "He didn't just say that."

"I believe he did." Gage's dad got him to do it again. "I thought he knew it already."

"I've been trying to teach him that and he would never say it. But, finally! Thank you, Quinn."

"My pleasure. See you all later. We have places to go and rooms to explore." He started toward the house with Josh babbling away.

"Hey, Dad, when will the lasagna be done?"

"You've got about thirty minutes."

"Thanks!" Way longer than he'd expected. This setup was too neatly choreographed. His dad and Kendra had deliberately arranged for him to be alone with Emma.

He turned to her. For the first time since she'd walked into the bakery, they were alone, and it was affecting his breathing and his heartbeat. "And then it was just us. Kind of freaky, huh?"

She took a deep breath. "Yes."

"Guess we should get started." He cleared his throat and adopted a formal tone. "The featured attractions for this official Wild Creek Ranch tour include the corral where the riding lessons take place, the pasture where the horses are turned out, the old historic barn where the family's horses are stabled, and the new barn where there are mostly boarders. What do you want to see first?"

"The old historic barn."

"Good choice." He hesitated. "Since this is a private tour, the guide would like to hold your hand."

She held it out. "I'd like that, too."

As he wove his fingers through hers and tightened his grip, warmth flowed up his arm and through his body. "Let's go."

_14_

Freaky was one word to describe the experience of strolling toward the old hip-roofed barn with Gage. Emma would go along with that description. But two others applied—exciting and liberating.

She'd hired a sitter for Josh a few times since he'd been born, but always for some obligatory thing like a dentist appointment. Never so that she could walk hand-in-hand with a handsome cowboy in the twilight.

Gage had worn a dove-gray yoked shirt that emphasized the width of this shoulders and the breadth of his chest. He'd also shaved, which he'd claimed had been for Josh's benefit. Maybe. And maybe he'd had a second motive.

"Do you know if Quinn and Kendra set this up on purpose?"

"I don't know, but if they did, I had nothing to do with it. I'm an innocent bystander."

She grinned. "Oh, yeah? Then why did you shave?"

"Like I said, for Josh."

She glanced at his profile. A crease in his freshly shaven cheek gave him away. "Uh-huh."

"And also on the off chance I might get a chance to kiss you again. I just didn't know when or where."

"That's what I thought." Heat shot through her body. The soft, gentle kiss he'd given her this afternoon had taunted her ever since. His restraint had been touching...and frustrating.

She'd experienced a fully involved Gage Sawyer kiss. The one in the Eagles Nest Market's parking lot had been like getting a sample of an ice cream flavor—so delicious she was tempted to ask for a full serving.

But did she dare indulge? That was the big question. As they approached the open double doors of the picturesque barn, her body warmed in anticipation. She hadn't kissed a man since Gage had ridden off into the sunset nineteen months ago.

Now that he was back in the picture, she was fantasizing about kisses and...maybe something more. She'd challenge any woman in her shoes not to.

He led her into the barn, fragrant with hay. "Usually they stick their heads out to see who's here, but as you can tell from all the chomping going on, they're too busy to care about us."

"Dinnertime, huh?"

"Yes, ma'am. What kind of experience have you had with horses?"

"I've watched the Budweiser Clydesdales on TV and I took Josh to the Fourth of July parade in Great Falls this summer."

"I see. You've never been on a horse?"

"Nope. But as I told Kendra today, I'd like to try it."

"That's good news. I think you'd have fun. I sure do. I'd like to teach Josh when he's old enough."

"When would that be?"

"If we're talking about putting him up there by himself, no sooner than four years old and more like five or six. But I could take him up with me now."

She sucked in a breath. "That scares me a little."

His smile was gentle. "Perfectly natural since you're not used to horses. No rush." He squeezed her hand. "Come on. I'll introduce you around." He paused next to a stall. "This is Strawberry, so named because he's a strawberry roan. Pete has a gelding named Clifford who looks something like this."

"What's a gelding?"

"A stallion who's been neutered. There's one mare named Licorice in this barn. The rest are all geldings. They make the best saddle horses."

"Huh." She studied the big horse as he munched away on the hay stuck in a wire basket attached to the stall. "He's very pretty."

"And such a sweetheart. If you decide to take a lesson, Kendra would likely put you on Strawberry."

Gage was close, very close. His warmth and the scent of his cologne surrounded her, awakening a response she hadn't experienced since...their last night together.

The air stirred as he moved away and came to a stop at the next stall. "This bay gelding is Jake. He has a very smooth gait, which is one of the reasons Zane uses him when he releases a raptor into the wild. Less jostling on the way out to the canyon."

The sensual undercurrent in his voice distracted her, making it difficult to focus on the conversation. Zane. Raptors. The rescue center they hoped to visit tomorrow. "It would be great if we can take Josh over to see those birds."

"It would be. My dad's artwork is in the lobby. Going there would be a twofer."

"Your dad's an artist? How did I miss that?"

"Probably because he doesn't go around talking about it. Selling the Lazy S has given him more time for his art and he's developed quite a following."

"I had no idea. That's wonderful._Is he a painter?"

"Scratchboard artist."

"What's that?"

"It's a little hard to explain. You'll see when we go to Raptors Rise. Glad you came down?"

She gazed at him. "Yes, I am."

"Me, too." Heat flickered in his dark eyes as he slowly lifted their joined hands and kissed the tips of her fingers.

The air left her lungs. He used to do that when...

"Emma, you're driving me crazy." He closed his eyes and sighed. "But we..." He paused to take a breath. "You need to meet Winston."

"Why?"

A piercing whinny filled the barn.

"There's your answer. He expects it."

"Alrighty, then."

Keeping a firm grip on her hand, Gage bypassed the other residents of the barn, who were still engrossed in their dinner. At the far end, a horse poked his head out of the stall. His dramatic coat was splashed with butterscotch and white.

"Oh, Gage, he's beautiful."

"Don't think he doesn't know it. Hey, Winston. Say hello to Emma."

The horse bobbed his head and made a throaty *huh-HUH-huh* sound.

"That almost sounds like hello!"

"Because it is his way of saying it." Gage reached across the stall door and stroked the horse's glossy neck. "He's named for Winston Churchill, and he's a talker. He's also the kingpin around here and if someone comes into the barn and doesn't pay attention to him, he lets that person know. Isn't that right, Winston?"

He snorted and tossed his head.

"He's fun to ride, too. Kendra's been generous enough to let me take him out a few times."

"You don't have a horse?"

"Used to. When I was ready to leave home, I knew I wouldn't be coming back except for visits. Didn't seem like Dad should be stuck feeding and exercising Sparrow. Didn't feel right to sell him." He scratched under Winston's flowing mane.

"I can understand that." The more he fondled the horse, the more her skin tingled.

"Sparrow was real gentle, so I donated him to an organization that teaches disabled kids to ride."

"What a great idea. Do you think you'll ever get another one?"

"I've thought about it. It's a commitment, though. Once you have a horse, you either take care of it every day or pay someone to do it. Ideally it should be you, so you bond with that animal. I do enjoy 'em, though." He looked over at her. "Want to stroke Winston's nose? It's like velvet. He loves being touched."

He's not the only one. She stepped closer and smoothed her hand down the horse's nose. "It does feel like velvet. Do you like this, Winston?"

He blew air softly through his nostrils.

"I think that's a yes. And now you can say you've made friends with a horse."

"Yeah." She continued to stroke Winston's nose. "This is kind of fun."

"You can branch out, reach up and scratch behind his ears, rub his neck."

"Like he's a big dog?"

"Exactly."

Winston did his low *huh-HUH-huh* thing again.

"He's telling you he likes that."

"I like it, too. His coat is so warm and smooth." She moved her hand in circles over his powerful neck.

"It is." He cleared his throat. "But you need to stop, now."

"Oh? Am I doing something wrong?" Turning her head, she met his gaze.

"Not wrong, but you're doing something...to me." Heat flared in his eyes.

Her hand stilled as her breathing kicked into high gear.

"Come on over here." He guided her away from the stall and into a secluded corner at the back of the barn. Releasing her hand, he slowly pulled her into his arms, his gaze never leaving hers. "I'm going to kiss you, Emma, and I hope to hell you feel like kissing me back, because I need..."

Her heart performed a quick drum solo and she couldn't seem to get enough air. "What...what do you need?"

He cradled the back of her head, splaying his fingers on either side of her ponytail. Then he leaned down until his mouth brushed hers. "You."

Her pulse leaped as he took full possession of her mouth. She kissed him back, all right. And then some.

The response she'd locked down since arriving yesterday burst forth, bubbling through her veins in a wild river of pleasure. Wrapping her arms around his neck, she reveled in the urgent press of his lips, the eager slide of his tongue, the erotic taste of his desire.

With a soft groan, he used both hands to cup her backside and tuck her in tight against his hips. There was no mistaking that move. He wanted more than a kiss.

So did she. The firm ridge of his cock brought everything back—the wild nights that had steamed up the windows of her bedroom and left her breathless and satisfied. The laughter and the pillow fights. Drinking cocoa in bed and experimenting with whipped cream...

He lifted his head and gulped for air. "We can't...we have to..."

"We have to go back to the house." She drew in a ragged breath. "How long have we been out here?"

"Damned if I know." His fingers flexed against the denim of her jeans. "And you're definitely in great shape."

She smiled. "We should have checked the time."

"Didn't think of it." He nuzzled the curve of her neck. "Too busy thinking about this."

Heaven. She tilted her head to give him greater access. "Admit it. You shaved for me."

"For both you and the baby." He nibbled her ear. "You taste delicious. Who needs dinner?"

"This isn't about dinner. We're Kendra's guests. We can't—"

"But I don't want to let you go."

"Mm." She closed her eyes. "But if one of us doesn't put a stop to this..."

"I will. Any minute, now." He dropped soft kisses all over her face.

"It's not like we can have sex."

"We can't?" He relaxed his grip and eased away from her. "I mean, I know not right now, but maybe later—"

"Later we'll have our little munchkin."

"Oh." He looked sheepish. "You're right. I'm not used to thinking in those terms." He heaved a sigh. "So this is it, then? A quick make-out session and back to being platonic for the rest of your visit?"

"It might be for the best."

He gazed at her. "Do you really think so?"

"I have no idea."

"That makes two of us." He recaptured her hand and squeezed it. "Let's go see about that munchkin."

15

Once Gage had a few brain cells working again, he questioned the wisdom of stealing those kisses in the barn. They only made him want more of what he couldn't have. Not during this visit, anyway.

Now there was a setup for sexual frustration. Good thing she was sitting across the dinner table, out of reach. It gave him a chance to cool down and refocus his attention on Josh.

The little guy was currently putting on a show gnawing away on one of the smaller pieces of corn. Clearly this wasn't Kendra's first rodeo. She'd put a vinyl tablecloth under the highchair at the end of the long table.

She and his dad sat on either side of Josh and supervised his meal. With Emma's permission, they gave him pieces of lettuce, a wedge of tomato and half of a dinner roll. He made a mess of all of it and a lot ended up on the vinyl cloth on the floor. They just laughed and gave him more ammunition.

Emma glanced across the table at Kendra. "I'm glad you had a cloth to put down."

"I'm glad I saved it. That thing's as old as Ryker." She gave Josh the other half of the dinner roll.

"Josh is an enthusiastic eater." Emma gazed at him with fondness. "And loves having an audience. Thanks for rising to the challenge and letting him interrupt your meal."

His dad turned to her and smiled. "It's a treat for me."

"Me, too," Kendra said. "It's like being the relievers for the starting pitcher. We're well rested and raring to go."

"Good description. And he's having the time of his life."

"Oh!" Kendra left her chair. "I have video of Grandpapa Quinn walking him through the house." She came back with her phone and handed it to Emma. "Take a look."

"I want to see this." Gage got up and walked around to peer over her shoulder. The scent of her perfume tempted him but he concentrated on the video. "Wow, Dad! You have him practically walking!"

"That's how I used to do it with you kids. Just get behind you and hold your hands. It works."

"We made it through the entire house," Kendra said. "He's seen the whole setup."

"Only time I picked him up was when I wanted him to look out the window so he could see the chicken coop. Too bad the chickens are tucked in for the night. I'll bet he'd have loved watching them." He turned to Josh. "Next time, little buddy."

"Pa-pa-pa-pa." Josh went back to mouthing the dinner roll.

"I would love to see them, too," Emma said. "Do you get fresh eggs?"

"I sure do." Kendra took back the phone when the video ended and scrolled through her pictures. "Here's the coop Trevor built for me."

"It's a Victorian house! How cool."

"It's a blast having chickens. I always wanted to."

"I'm sure Josh would be excited to see them. Like I said, he's having the time of his life. Gage talked about taking him for a short horseback ride, too."

"With me holding him, of course." Gage returned to his seat. "Just a short circuit around the pasture."

Kendra nodded. "I did that with all my boys. Got 'em used to horses from the time they could sit up."

"I did the same," his dad said. "Great idea to start Josh on it now, son." He turned to Emma. "Maybe I could talk you into driving over to my place in the morning. Gage can saddle up one of our horses and that way I can—"

"But Dad, you work in your studio every morning. It's your special time."

"And that's important, but this little shaver is leaving on Monday and tomorrow is filling up."

"It is?" That was news to him.

"Yep. Kendra, did you tell them about the raptor center?"

"Whoops. Forgot. Zane said you could come over around eleven. Does that work?"

"Sure does," Emma said. "Thank you for arranging it."

"Anyway," his dad continued. "After the raptor center you'll want to head to the soda fountain for a sandwich and a hot fudge sundae. Then Josh will need a nap, and poof! The day's gone. I can forgo a couple of hours in my studio in the morning if the payoff is seeing my grandson sit a horse for the first time."

Gage looked over at Emma. "What do you think?"

"I think that would be wonderful. He's a lucky boy. It's like a grandkid's paradise around here."

Kendra beamed at her. "I was hoping you thought so, because I have a huge request."

"What's that?"

"Quinn and I would love to keep him tomorrow night. Quinn's already shown him the crib he'd sleep in, and if you bring him a little early he can help me feed the chickens, and we can take him down to the barn, and sit on the front porch for a while, and—"

"You can tell she's not very excited about this plan," his dad said with a smile.

Emma looked startled. "You mean overnight?"

"If you'd consider it," Kendra said. "You and Gage could go out for a nice dinner at the Guzzling Grizzly. Nicole will be performing tomorrow night and she does this singalong thing that is really popular."

"It's amazing." Gage hurried to add his two cents. "The energy of the place shoots up about a thousand percent when everyone joins in on the old country favorites." He focused on Emma. "I guarantee you'd have fun."

"I've never left him overnight before."

"There's always a first time." Kendra's voice was warm with understanding. "And you'd make Quinn and me really happy. What a pleasure to have him all to ourselves."

"Well...I guess it's not like we'd be out of touch. I'd have my phone with me and you could call or text if anything came up."

"And we would," his dad said. "Instantly. I promise you we wouldn't try to wing it."

Emma smiled. "Considering the combined parental experience you and Kendra bring to the task, you'd probably handle an emergency better than I would."

His heart beat faster. She was seriously considering the idea. Which could mean...better not let himself go there. It could show in his expression. Maintain. Maintain.

"And like Kendra says, there's got to be a first time and who better than you two?" Emma took a breath. "It would be a good thing for both Josh and me. Thank you. I accept."

Gage worked very hard to mute his response. Even so, his exclamation of "Great!" was likely too enthusiastic if his dad's raised eyebrows were any indication.

The meal ended soon after that. The combination of a long day and a short nap had finally caught up with Josh. He could barely keep his eyes open.

Gage carried him out to Emma's car and the baby was asleep by the time he was belted in. "I think we wore him out today."

"You know, that's okay." Emma stowed the baby backpack on the floor of the car and softly closed the door. "His world has just expanded and I couldn't be happier about that."

"What time should I have a horse saddled in the morning?"

"How about nine? That gives me plenty of time to get us both ready for the day. Besides, Mrs. Stanislowski told me that Sunday breakfast is the highlight of the week at the B&B."

"You don't want to miss that." He'd contact Mrs. Stanislowski in the morning and make sure she had his credit card on file to take care of Emma's bill.

"I'm touched that your dad will change his work schedule for this."

"Which tells you just how badly he wants to do it."

"I can tell, which is one of the reasons I went along with the idea. The first time Josh *sits a horse* as your dad phrased it, must be a big deal."

"You've got that right. The family photo albums have a picture of each of us on that day. It's not like we had to do anything except sit in my dad's lap, but the significance of it was huge."

"I'm getting that. This might be more important than Josh's first solo steps."

"It is to horse people. It's the passing of the torch."

"Then Josh is supposed to grow up to be a cowboy? If I pay attention to that old song, I shouldn't let him."

"Yeah, well." Gage smiled. "It's a great song but I can't go along with the message. Josh could do worse than a career working with horses."

"I'll keep that in mind." She made a movement to go. "I should probably get that little guy home."

"Right." He walked with her around to the driver's door. "It appears we have a date for tomorrow night." He said it casually, as if he hadn't pinned all kinds of hopes on that event.

"Guess so." She turned to him. "You sounded happy about that."

He didn't have enough light to see her expression. "I am happy. How about you?"

"It should be fun if I'm not on pins and needles worrying about how Josh is doing."

"Then I'll just have to keep you thoroughly entertained, won't I?"

She tossed her keys from one hand to the other. "Think you're up to it, cowboy?"

She was in. Excitement left him breathless. "Yes, ma'am, I do."

"Are you sure about that? You've only given me one real kiss since I got here. How do I know whether you can deliver on your—*mmph.*"

He kissed her for all he was worth, holding her steady with a firm grasp on her shoulders. The sweet connection with her mouth flooded his body with heat that arrowed straight to his bad boy.

As her lips softened beneath his, as she moaned and opened to the thrust of his tongue, joy rushed though him. He'd driven to Great Falls two days ago because of this...transcendence.

Sinking into a kiss with Emma meant surrendering to the magic of something he couldn't quite explain. He'd only found it with her.

They'd been good together, the best. Neither of them had been ready to admit it. Maybe they weren't ready now, either. He needed more time alone with her, much more time. Tomorrow night would be a start but he already knew it wouldn't be enough.

* * *

The next morning at breakfast with his dad and Pete, Gage discussed which of the three horses in the barn would be best for Josh's first experience.

"Any of them." Pete ate his last piece of bacon. "Too bad you don't have a horse out there, bro, since I assume you'll be the one doing the honors."

"He will," their dad said. "That's tradition. I'm not saying I wouldn't love to do it, but I've had my turn, four times."

"Then which horse do you think I should saddle up?"

"I agree with Pete. They're all sweethearts and would be reliable. But since you don't have a horse of your own, how about using mine? Then we'll memorialize Banjo in a picture as well as Josh's first time."

Gage smiled. "I was thinking that, too. A buckskin will be a little different. As I recall, we have a lot of bays in those photo albums." He pushed away his plate. "That reminds me. Do you have the old photo albums handy?"

"In a box in my closet. I've considered getting some of those pictures digitized before they get any more faded. Did you want to have a look at the one of you on a horse when you were a little squirt?"

"I was thinking about it. Emma might get a kick out of seeing me when I was around Josh's age."

"Then I'll dig that one out for you." He left the table and carried his dishes to the sink. "It'll take me a while to find the right album." He opened the dishwasher and put his plate in. "So you and Pete should go on out to the barn."

"We'll do that. Is Kendra coming over?"

"Yep. She said she'd get here as soon as she could." He closed the dishwasher and left the kitchen.

Pete finished his coffee and put down his mug. "We do have a lot of bays in those family pictures, now that you mention it."

"Because they're popular. Wes chose one."

"And I picked Clifford partly because he's a strawberry roan and I wanted something different. Do you ever regret giving away Sparrow?"

"No. He didn't fit my lifestyle and he was perfectly suited to that program."

"What about now?"

"Emma asked if I planned to get another one. I told her I was thinking about it. They do tie a person down, though."

"So does a kid."

He met his brother's gaze. "I'm aware of that. It's one of the reasons I'm not rushing out to get a horse."

"Yeah, although…"

"What?"

"Never mind." He stood and picked up his dishes. "Let's go get that buckskin ready for his close-up."

_16_

Emma slowed the car as she came to the end of a winding dirt road and her tires crunched on a circular gravel drive. Although Quinn's house wasn't as large and impressive as Kendra's, Emma liked it instantly.

Maybe it was the warm brown shade of the wood exterior and the rustic look of the wooden shutters. The rockers sat slightly askew on the front porch and a magazine lay on a nearby table, as if someone had just left to refill a coffee mug. Tall, feathery pines grew close to the house and several small birds hopped around on the porch floor as if searching for crumbs.

Sparrows? Gage had named his horse after a small bird, not an eagle or a hawk. She was curious about that choice.

She stopped in front of the house and looked across a clearing toward the barn, where all the action was taking place. Three pickups, including Gage's, were parked to one side of the double door.

The hitching post on the other side was the focus of all the activity. Quinn had a rag in his hand and looked to be polishing the coat of a caramel-colored horse. It had a black mane and tail. Its legs were black, too, making it seem as if it wore stockings.

Pete was combing the long, graceful tail, which nearly reached the ground. Then he finished that and went to get a small, colorful blanket that was draped over the hitching post. Quinn stepped back as Pete flipped the blanket onto the horse's back.

At the same time, Gage came out of the barn carrying a saddle. She laughed. He wore a child-sized cowboy hat secured under his chin with a string. Somehow he'd come up with one for Josh and evidently had decided putting it on was the best way to keep it handy. Goofy guy.

He lifted the saddle onto the horse's back and turned to wave, motioning her to drive down. Then he grabbed a wide strap attached to the saddle and ducked under the horse's belly. She knew nothing about saddles, but this one looked fancy. Silver trim sparkled in the sunlight.

Josh began rocking his seat and humming. Time to drive that kid over to his initiation into the world of cowboys. His blue and white striped shirt looked more nautical than Western, but at least the floppy canvas hat he wore would be replaced with something more appropriate.

She parked on the far side of the line of trucks. By the time she'd lifted Josh out of his car seat, Gage had arrived.

"Great timing. We're almost ready."

She glanced at him and grinned. "Interesting look you have going on."

"Tell me the truth, now. Does this hat make my head look fat?"

"Well, since you've asked…"

"Yeah, I had a hunch." He took it off. "Hey, sport, see what Daddy has for you!"

"Da-da!" Josh reached out both arms.

"Pretty cool, huh? Wanna try it on, see if it fits?"

"It looks about right." Emma balanced him on her hip while she took off the canvas one. "Luckily he's used to hats."

"If he likes it, I'll get him one that's similar, since he can't keep this one. It's a family heirloom, designated for first ride photo shoots."

"Then we'd better make sure he doesn't chew on it."

"Da-da-da-da!" Josh wiggled with excitement as Gage hunkered down.

"He shouldn't get a chance if he's wearing it. Hold still, buddy. This needs to go at the right angle."

Josh blew a raspberry at him.

"No, I'm not kidding. The tilt of a guy's hat is very important. Let's tug the brim down a little. There. Now you look like you mean business."

Emma giggled.

"Never mind your mama. It's a guy thing." He glanced up as a white van drove past the house and parked next to Emma's SUV. "And here's Granny Ken, just in time to take your picture. Okay, gonna tighten the string under your chin and…we're done!"

Kendra came around the back of her van, phone in hand. "Oh, my God. Super cute! Quinn, you should get over here and see this!"

"Be right there!"

"*So* adorable." Kendra raised her phone and took several shots. "Can I put this on the town website, Emma?"

"Sure." She looked at Quinn as he hurried over. "Thank you for letting Josh wear the family heirloom."

"He's family." His face creased in a wide smile. "And he looks great. I'm glad I found the hat."

"What do you mean, *found it*?" Gage looked at him. "You didn't know where it was?"

"Nope. Stumbled across it when I got out the boxes I'd used to pack the photo albums. I'd tucked the hat inside the first one. I wasn't even sure you'd want Josh to wear it."

"Why wouldn't I?"

"It's seen better days. When I was cleaning things out at the Lazy S, I debated whether to give it to Goodwill."

"You're kidding." Gage turned to Pete, who was on his way over with his black hat.

"Did you know Dad almost gave our baby cowboy hat to Goodwill?"

"No, I did not know that." He handed Gage his Stetson. "Hey, Dad, why would you get rid of a family heirloom?"

He shrugged. "It's showing its age. Bet I could find a new one that looks just like it in about five minutes online."

"That's a terrible idea. You don't get rid of an important piece of family history because it's a little beat up. Maybe I should be the guardian of this hat."

Quinn smiled. "Be my guest."

"Good plan, bro," Gage said. "You can take possession after Josh wears it for his picture. Is Banjo ready?"

"I've done about all the grooming on that animal I can think of short of giving him a mani-pedi and an herbal wrap."

"Alrighty, then." He glanced at Josh. "Whatcha say, buckaroo? Ready to ride?"

"Da-da!"

"Excellent." He lifted him into his arms. "Got your phone, Emma?"

She took it out of her purse and held it up.

"Dad? Got yours?"

Quinn pulled his from his back pocket.

"Then let's get 'er done." With Pete at his side, he started toward the horse tethered to the hitching post.

Emma walked with Quinn and Kendra as they followed the brothers.

"Can't tell you how much this means to me," Quinn said. "Seeing my grandson on a horse for the first time is a thrill."

"I'm glad it's worked out. Is that saddle as valuable as it looks?"

"It's priceless. My kids went together on it for my fiftieth birthday."

"Well, it's gorgeous. Is Banjo your horse?"

"Yes, ma'am. He's been with me quite a while, now. The only buckskin I've ever had. He's a good one."

"Gentle?"

"Sure is. Otherwise I wouldn't allow him near my grandbaby." He looked over at her. "And neither would Gage."

She nodded, unable to get any words past the sudden lump in her throat. Two days ago, none of these folks had even known Josh existed. Now they were treating him like the most precious being on the planet. She'd won the lottery without even realizing she was playing.

That knowledge went a long way to easing her anxiety about her little boy approaching the very big horse.

Gage stopped a few feet away from Banjo and talked quietly with Josh, whose gaze was riveted on the horse.

The horse turned his head toward them and Josh bounced in Gage's arms, squealing with excitement. Gage continued talking quietly and Josh settled down. Only then did Gage move closer.

His measured approach calmed her nerves. He might be new at this daddy business, but he clearly had a talent for it. He'd already mastered the art of soothing his son when the occasion called for it.

He continued talking to Josh as he brought him within touching distance and helped the baby stroke the horse's neck. Kendra and Quinn lifted their phones to take pictures, but she couldn't bear to look away long enough to turn on her phone's camera. She might miss something.

Pete took charge of Josh while Gage untied the horse and mounted up. Leaning down, he scooped Josh out of Pete's arms and onto his lap. Other than a soft little *oh* of surprise, Josh sat quietly, his eyes wide as he peeked out from under the brim of the brown cowboy hat.

"Atta-boy, Gage," Quinn murmured as he continued taking pictures. "Nicely done."

The obvious pride in his voice made Emma smile. "He's doing a fabulous job."

Holding Josh firmly with one arm around his tummy, Gage laid the reins against the buckskin's neck and turned the horse to face them. "This is it, guys," he said. "The money shot."

That galvanized Emma into action. She gave her attention to her phone long enough to activate the camera before holding it up and focusing on Gage and Josh.

The image that filled the screen made her heart swell with love for her son, who'd accepted the unfamiliar hat without complaint and had trusted a man he'd known for two days to keep him safe on top of a very large animal.

As for that broad-shouldered cowboy, he looked every inch the proud daddy as he sat astride a powerful horse with his infant son. The image touched her, burrowing deep. Because of Josh, Gage would always own a piece of her heart.

Tucking Josh in close, he leaned over. The black Stetson obscured his face as he murmured something to the little boy.

Josh's lips moved, but he was talking very softly, probably mimicking Gage's lowered volume.

"A little louder, buddy." Gage looked up. "Emma, can you come closer? I think you'll want to hear this."

She approached the horse with some hesitation. There was no stall door between her and the animal like there had been with Winston.

The mustang stood very still and gazed at her with liquid brown eyes. She could at least be as brave as her son. She drew near enough that she could have reached out and stroked his nose, but she chose not to.

"Okay, Josh." Gage dipped his head again. "Just like you've been doing. Ma-ma."

The sound came out as a baby whisper that could have been anything. Emma smiled. "That's sweet, but you don't have to—"

"He's been saying it, though. When I was calming him down I told him *let's make your mama proud.* Repeated it a few times. Then he started saying ma-ma. Come on, sport. Ma-ma."

Josh looked right at her and spoke in a clear voice. "Ma-ma."

Her breath caught. "Oh, *Josh.*"

Gage glanced up. "Now don't tell me he doesn't know what he's saying."

"I absolutely won't." She met his gaze. "What a gift. Thank you."

"Thought you'd like that." He flashed her a smile. "Now, if you'll excuse us, we're going to take a short ride around the pasture. Be back in a few."

He turned the horse and rode slowly toward the gate Pete had just opened.

"Come on, Emma." Kendra linked an arm through hers. "Let's go watch."

"I wouldn't miss it for the world."

17

Josh's first time on a horse had gone well, thank God. Gage had been determined it would, but nothing was guaranteed in this world, was it? After he'd made one successful circuit of the pasture, his dad had excused himself to go work in his studio and Kendra had headed home to do chores.

But Uncle Pete had been eager to assume his new role. He'd wanted to show Emma and Josh around the place and introduce them to his horse Clifford and Wes's horse Fudge. Then he'd helped Gage improvise a high chair so Emma could feed Josh the lunch she'd brought.

They'd stacked cushions on a straight-backed chair, used one of Gage's belts to secure the baby, and pushed him up to the kitchen table. Worked like a charm. After Josh finished his early lunch, Emma had given them a lesson in diaper changing. They'd cheerfully pitched in, to her apparent surprise.

In the end, he'd run out of time to show her the photo album his dad had unearthed. They'd had to leave for their tour of Raptors Rise. No worries. Emma would be back the following weekend for Josh's birthday party. That would be the perfect time to share it with her.

On the way out the door, she suggested that he ride with her, which made sense. He strapped Josh in his car seat, climbed in the passenger side, and off they went.

Another first. He'd never ridden in a vehicle with her. The intimacy of it struck him. He glanced over to see whether she was the least bit agitated by it.

Didn't seem to be. Her cheeks were their usual creamy color. With her hair swept back in a ponytail, he could admire the soft curve of her neck where he'd placed several kisses the previous evening. And would place even more tonight barring something unexpected. His groin tightened.

When they were with other people, he managed to ignore the glittering prospect of having her to himself. But in the confines of this car, he was *almost* alone with her, and—

"You and Pete handled that diaper change with a refreshing lack of drama."

Now there was a subject guaranteed to deflate his enthusiasm along with a significant body part. "We muck out stalls for a living. Squeamish wranglers don't last long."

"I hadn't factored that in. I guess your job requires you to be indifferent to the earthier aspects of life."

"I wouldn't go that far."

"Meaning?"

"Some of the earthier aspects are meant to be enjoyed. I would hate to become indifferent to those."

Sunglasses covered her eyes but her pink cheeks gave her away. "Gage..."

"Come on, Emma, you have to be thinking about it."

"Well, I am, but overlaying that is the reality of leaving my son overnight for the first time ever."

"It's a big step. I probably don't even understand how big since I haven't been taking care of him for almost a year."

"But I couldn't ask for two better people to leave him with. My rational side knows that he'll be fine, but my emotional side is—"

"See, that's where I come in." Time to shift the topic to something a little juicier.

"You mean by distracting me."

"Exactly. And we might want to consider changing the dinner plan."

"The singalong at the Guzzling Grizzly? You don't want to do that?"

"I'd be happy to do that, but I can't guarantee you'll be sufficiently distracted."

"Yeah, maybe not. Singing along with Nicole could remind me of singing to Josh in the car and I'll be toast."

"On the other hand, I know one sure-fire way I can take your mind off Josh." He paused to let that sink in. "But it would get us thrown out of the restaurant."

She didn't say a word. She didn't have to. Her blush and her quick gulp communicated her state of mind perfectly.

"So I'm thinking instead of going out, we should pick up some food and go back to the B&B. I'm fairly certain that if we do that, I should be able to—"

"Stop talking about it." Her words were rushed and she squirmed in her seat.

"Why?" He gave her a slow smile. "Am I getting you hot?"

"Never mind. We'll decide on dinner later. We're here." She swung the SUV into the empty parking area. Gripping the wheel, she drew in a shaky breath.

"You might want to shut off the motor."

"Right." She switched off the engine.

"Did I take your mind off Josh?"

"Yes, you did." She took another deep breath. "Now I have to get my mind off you."

"Just testing." Reaching over, he cupped her chin and turned her toward him. Then he gently pulled off her sunglasses. His pulse rate spiked at the heat in her gaze. "What a shame if we get to the moment of truth and discover we can't blot out the world like we did before."

She swallowed. "I don't think that'll be a problem."

"Good." Leaning over, he brushed his lips over hers. "Now let's show that little guy some eagles." Handing her back her glasses, he climbed out of the car and went to free Josh from his car seat.

Emma wanted him as much as ever. Hallelujah for that. The intensity of the moment in the car eased as he picked up the baby and walked with Emma into the facility, but he remained in a state of heightened awareness. Judging from the way she kept sneaking looks at him, she was in the same condition.

The lobby was empty. With no one in there, she'd have an unobstructed view of his dad's artwork and he was eager for her to see it. She couldn't miss it since it dominated one wall.

When she spotted it, she gasped. "That's your dad's?"

"Sure is." How great to be able to say that, to be the son of Quinn Sawyer. The life-sized image of a family of bald eagles in a massive tree-top nest gave him a shiver of pride no matter how many times he saw it. His dad had named it *Home, Sweet Home.*

"That's *amazing.* You told me the name of the technique before. What was it?"

"It's called scratchboard." Josh wiggled with excitement and chanted *ba-ba* as he carried him a little closer to get a better look. "Dad can explain it better than I can, but he starts with a dry surface coated with black ink. Then he scratches the image into it to create...this."

"Incredible. And what a perfect choice of subject for a town called Eagles Nest. I'm sure that was no accident."

"Actually, it was. Wildlife is his passion and he was intrigued by the challenge of an intricate nest and getting the feathers just right on a life-sized piece. But as he worked on it, he realized he couldn't sell it to an individual. It belonged on permanent display somewhere in town. This was the logical place."

"Lucky me, that he decided to donate it to us." Zane walked into the lobby from a nearby corridor. "Hey, Emma and Gage. Glad you could bring Josh over."

Emma turned. "Thanks for letting us come before you open. Once I heard about this place I couldn't wait to see it. And Josh is fascinated with birds."

Zane smiled. "Takes after his dad?"

Gage returned the smile. "Maybe. In any case, seeing those eagles should be epic for him."

"Hope so. How did his first ride go?"

Emma looked surprised. "You knew about that?"

"Yes, ma'am. I was over at the ranch early this morning helping Mom feed the horses. She couldn't talk about anything else. She said you're letting her babysit tonight and she's so excited."

"It'll be my first time leaving him overnight, so I'm a little nervous."

"Understandable. So, ready to get this show on the road?"

Emma nodded. "Absolutely."

"I recommend we do it a little differently than I normally would because this one's for Josh. We need to go for the gee-whiz stuff outside instead of the indoor facilities."

"I agree," Gage said. "He'll be mainly interested in the birds out in the enclosures."

"That's what I figured. Anyway, we don't have any birds in the infirmary right now, thank goodness, and the nursery is empty this time of year. We'll go straight outside."

Emma walked along with him. "You have a nursery?"

"Yes, ma'am. Spring and summer, for orphaned raptors. You should come back then so you can see it in action."

"I'd love to."

Zane led them down a paved path to the screened-in shelters for injured birds of prey. Each was as large as Zane's budget would permit and shaded by trees to give the birds the privacy to heal. Gage had taken the full tour soon after arriving in town and had been back several times since.

"Now that we have more space," Zane said, "we've divided the birds into groups – hawks, eagles and owls. Which do you want Josh to see first?"

"Eagles," Emma said. "I think he'll be blown away. I can't wait for his reaction."

"I'll take the pictures this time." Gage walked over to her. "That way you can share the experience with him."

"But you and Josh are the bird lovers. I'll have fun watching you two communing with them. You take him and I'll handle pictures."

"Alrighty, then." He glanced at Zane. "I guess we're ready to do this thing."

He nodded. "Follow me."

Gage repositioned Josh in his arms and adjusted the fit of his floppy canvas hat. "All set, buddy?"

Josh reached up and patted his cheek. "Da-da."

"You bet I am, buddy. We're gonna go see some eagles, now." As he followed Zane and Emma, he lowered his voice to a soft murmur. "They've been hurt and they shouldn't be agitated. I need you to be very, very quiet. Can you do that for me?"

Josh gazed up at him, his brown eyes solemn. His voice was like the whisper of the wind through the pines over their heads. "Da-da."

His chest tightened. This little kid, not even a year old, appeared to understand his request. He'd bet his black hat that Josh wasn't going to disturb those birds.

And he didn't. Gage brought him within inches of the wire mesh separating him from a magnificent bald eagle with a badly injured foot. As Emma pointed her phone in their direction, Josh and the eagle stared at each other, neither moving, neither making a sound, simply exchanging mutual respect.

The pattern was repeated with each of the large birds. Josh regarded them quietly and they returned the favor. Same with the hawks and the owls. The pygmy owl could have stirred him up since it was about the size of his plush bluebird. But other than softly mouthing *ba-ba*, he gave the tiny owl the same consideration as its larger cousins.

When they returned to the lobby, Zane glanced at Josh. "I've seen quite a few kids go through here and none of them have been that quiet and respectful."

Gage smiled at his son. "We had an agreement, didn't we, sport?"

Josh grinned, showing off all four teeth.

18

"That was amazing. And I got some fabulous videos." Emma put the SUV in gear, backed out of the parking spot and headed for the main road into town.

"I was hoping you did. He was so damn cute staring intently at those birds while they stared right back at him."

"He was fascinated. And now, to top it off, he gets his first visit to an old-fashioned soda fountain. The fun just never stops for that kid."

"For me, either. Seeing things through his eyes is a trip. I love it. Oh, and I just thought of another good reason to go to Pills and Pop today. Ellie Mae Stockton will be there. She's a hoot and a half."

She smiled at his enthusiasm. "She works there?"

"As a clerk. She's in her eighties. Thoroughly enjoys the job."

"I can't wait to meet her."

"You'll like her. She wears classic outfits like in a forties movie. She says she used to be in the film industry. According to her, she works Sundays so employees with families don't have to, but I also think she has a crush on Hank. He's retired, but he fills in at the soda fountain every Sunday."

"Or maybe it's the other way around and Hank's there because he has a crush on her."

"Maybe. He's a good twenty years younger that she is, but Ellie Mae's ageless, so it could work. Check it out while we're there and see what you think."

"I will. In between bites of my hot fudge sundae."

"But we're getting sandwiches first, right?"

She'd had time to consider what he'd said about the evening ahead and she was ready to lay her cards on the table. "The thing is, Mrs. Stanislowski put on quite a spread for breakfast. I was thinking of just getting the sundae and I could order a sandwich to eat…" She paused for dramatic effect. "Later."

He sucked in a quick breath that sent him into a coughing fit. Eventually he cleared his throat and turned to her. "How much later?"

"Oh, I don't know." She managed to keep a straight face. "Whenever I get hungry. Could be dinnertime. Could be later. It all depends on what's happening."

"I see." He cleared his throat again. "That sounds like a great idea."

"Might not work for you, though. You're probably hungry now."

He groaned softly. "Count on it."

"Payback, my friend."

"Trust me, it's worth every pinch on my privates. I'm crazy about this plan."

"Figured you would be." She parked in front of the vintage drugstore.

"But if you wouldn't mind fetching Josh out of his seat while I take a few restorative breaths, I'd be most appreciative."

"Be happy to." She allowed herself a tiny smirk as she climbed out and went around to the other side where Josh was rocking in his seat, eager to get out. "You're in for a treat, kiddo. Mommy's going to let you taste her hot fudge sundae."

"Ma-ma!"

"Oh, sweetie, how I love hearing you say that." She lifted him out and nudged the door shut. "And I have your daddy to thank for it."

The passenger door opened and Gage emerged. He gave her a crooked grin. "Howdy, ma'am. Nice-looking kid you have there."

"If you think he's cute, you should see his daddy."

"I happen to know that ugly cuss and I guarantee this baby got his looks from his mama. Can I take him, now?"

"If you're up to it."

"I'm fine, thanks." He took charge of Josh. "But please don't be offended if I ignore you while you eat your ice cream. I'm liable to put an erotic spin on that activity and then I'll be forced to go back to the car."

"Poor Gage."

"Oh, yeah, I'm in misery. But that's okay, because I know you'll make it up to me later."

"You seem quite sure about that."

"Yes, ma'am. The sandwich suggestion clinched it." He grinned. "You want me bad."

Whew. That smile knocked her for a loop. She was a tad bit wobbly as she walked with him over to the drugstore's front door. She'd forgotten how accomplished he was at this sexual teasing business. She needed a chance to catch her breath.

And this was the perfect place to do it. Pills and Pop delighted her from the moment she stepped through the door. Black and white tiles on the floor, neon signs on the wall and a counter with red vinyl and chrome stools made the place look like a fifties movie set. A family with three little kids occupied a booth in the corner and a couple of teenage girls were drinking chocolate shakes at the counter.

"What a great place, Gage."

"Ooo, I adore it whenever someone has that reaction." A woman in a knee-length gray skirt, heels and a white silk blouse came toward them. "I'm going to take a wild guess that you're Emma and this cutie in the canvas hat is Josh."

Emma smiled at her. "And I'm going to take a wild guess that you're Ellie Mae Stockton."

"In the flesh!" She thrust out a slim hand. "I see my reputation has preceded me. Pleased to meet you, Emma. You and Josh are the talk of the town."

"It appears that my reputation has preceded me, too." Emma shook her hand. Ellie Mae had a firm grip. "Is being the talk of the town good or bad?"

"Oh, good, always good. It's far better to make waves than be irrelevant. Excuse me a moment." She turned toward the family in the booth as they got up to leave. "Bye, now! Thanks for coming in!"

"We loved it!" the woman called out as they headed for the door.

"They always do." Ellie Mae shifted her attention back to Emma, Gage and Josh. "That's the joy of working here. Did you come to eat or shop?"

Emma said *eat* at the same moment Gage said *both.* She looked at him. "What do we need to shop for?"

He held her gaze.

"Oh." Condoms. If they were going to pick up where they'd left off, they'd need those little raincoats, and she certainly didn't have any with her.

Not that those things were foolproof. He was holding the evidence in his arms. Regardless, she was willing to put her trust in that item and he'd wisely figured out now was the time to purchase it.

"But we can head over to the soda fountain first," Gage said, "and get our order going."

"Good idea." Emma glanced at Ellie Mae, who seemed highly amused by the subtext clearly involved. "We're having hot fudge sundaes."

"Of course you are." She leaned closer to Josh. "And how about you, little man? What are you having?"

Josh blew a raspberry right in her face.

Before Emma could apologize, Ellie Mae blew one right back at him and they both laughed.

"I love kids." She turned to Emma. "I can't imagine having any of my own, though. I just like messing with them when they come in. But enough jibber-jabbering. Let's get you over to the soda fountain so Hank can fix you up." She headed in that direction. "Hey, Hank, sweetie, you have customers itching for your famous hot fudge sundaes."

"I'm locked and loaded, Ellie Mae." The guy behind the counter was a burly sixty-something man with a thick head of gray hair and kind eyes. "Hi, there, Gage."

"Greetings, Hank. I'd like you to meet Emma Green and our son Josh."

Hank smiled. "Pleased to meet you, ma'am. That's a mighty fine baby you two have."

Ellie Mae beamed at them. "Isn't he, though? Look at those eyes, big as saucers."

"He's never seen anything like this," Emma said. "All the shiny chrome and the neon. The jukebox is awesome."

"That's original," Hank said. "The owner's been lucky enough to find people who could locate replacement parts to keep it running."

"Come on, Josh." Gage fished change out of his pocket and started toward the jukebox. "What song do you want? Something by Garth Brooks? Reba McEntyre?"

"Ba-ba!" Josh pointed at the glowing machine.

"He loves *Boot Scootin' Boogie*," Emma said.

"Brooks and Dunn it is, then." Gage dropped money in the slot and punched a button. Then he glanced over at Emma. "Do you know the dance?"

"I do. Do you?"

"Yes, ma'am."

"I know the dance," Ellie Mae said.

"We know the dance," piped up one of the teenagers.

"I'll be the audience." Hank leaned against the counter.

Gage flashed Emma a smile. "Then let's do it."

Laughing, she jumped in next to him. Ellie Mae lined up next to her and the teenagers moved in behind them as the music started. The black and white checkered dance area was just big enough for five people and a baby to execute the steps.

Josh spent the entire dance giggling and bouncing in time to the music. Emma loused up and went the wrong way twice because she was so busy watching Josh's face and Gage's tush. That cowboy had moves.

When the song ended, Hank applauded their efforts. The teenagers fussed over Josh for a while before they left. Then Ellie Mae had to go greet arriving customers.

Emma glanced at Gage. "Sundae time?"

"You betcha."

"I can hold Josh for a while."

"No worries. I've got him." He settled on a stool with Josh in his lap.

Hank smiled at them. "I know you want hot fudge sundaes, but around here we make 'em to order. Emma, how do you like yours?"

"With plenty of fudge, whipped cream and nuts, please. No maraschino cherry, though. I know it's traditional, but I'm not crazy about them."

"How about a fresh strawberry instead?"

"That would work. Thanks!"

"You're most welcome. A sundae needs a spot of color on the top." He turned to Gage. "How about you?"

"Exactly the same, please. A strawberry on top suits me, too."

"How about Josh?"

"I'll give him a few bites of mine," Emma said.

"Then sit tight. You'll be savoring your sundaes before you know it." He took a couple of tall glass sundae dishes from a shelf and flipped up a polished chrome lid covering a tub of vanilla ice cream.

Emma glanced over at Gage. "Let me have him for a minute. I want to do something."

"Okay. Incoming!" Lifting Josh, he zoomed him around, making a noise like an airplane.

Josh squealed with delight.

"And it's a perfect three-point landing!" Gage settled the laughing baby in her lap.

"Oh, my goodness, Josh!" She hugged him tight. "You were flying!"

"Da-da!"

"I know! Daddy's magic, isn't he?"

"Better believe it."

"Oh, I do." She gave him a quick smile. "But Mommy's magic, too. She can make you go round and round." With her arm anchoring him against her ribs, she grabbed the counter and pushed. The stool slowly revolved.

Josh let out a soft little *ohhh.*

Gage chuckled. "You should see his face. He's really thinking about that one."

"Want to do it again, only faster?"

He bounced in her lap. "Ma-ma!"

"Then here goes..." She pushed harder.

The stool whipped around once and Josh squealed. When the next revolution was slower, he repeated that awed little *ohhh.*

"Oh, man." Gage looked totally besotted by his son. "Major cuteness going on. I don't know how you get anything done during the day when the alternative is playing with Josh."

"It's a challenge."

"I'll bet. I—hey, looks like our sundaes are on the way."

Hank set one in front of each of them. "*Bon appetit.*"

"Oh, Hank." Emma glanced up at him. "Those are spectacular."

"I still get a kick out of putting them together, even after all these years."

Josh made a grab for hers and she held him back. "Easy does it, champ." Picking up her spoon, she dipped it in the whipped cream and offered it to him.

He leaned forward and slurped it right up.

Gage laughed. "Now there's an endorsement. How about if I take him back for this part? I've had a chance to enjoy Hank's sundaes before but you haven't. And if I hold him, you can give him small tastes easier."

"That's a fine idea. I accept."

They were in the middle of that program when Ellie Mae came back. "I can tell Josh is excited about that sundae. Want a video of you feeding it to him?"

"I'd love it." Emma stuck her spoon in her sundae and dug her phone out of the small shoulder purse she'd laid on the counter. She handed it to Ellie Mae. "Someone's first hot fudge sundae should be recorded for posterity."

"My thought exactly." Ellie Mae moved back and held up the phone. "Hank, get in the picture. That way they'll have a record of the creator of those sundaes."

"Where should I be?"

"Behind the counter like you are, but if you move so you're right between Emma and Gage, then I can get all four of you more easily. *There* you go. Like that. Emma, are you ready to feed Josh another spoonful?"

"I am."

"Perfect. Action.! Rolling."

Emma managed not to giggle. Whether or not Ellie Mae had been in the film industry, she'd picked up some lingo. The video would be one more souvenir of this memorable weekend.

She and Gage put in their sandwich order while they were finishing their sundaes and he managed to slip away long enough to buy the condoms. By the time the sundaes were gone, Josh was fading. Emma coaxed him into waving bye-

bye to Hank and Ellie Mae, but after that, he was done.

As she carried her sleepy boy to the SUV, Gage hurried ahead and opened the back door for her. She tucked Josh into his car seat and walked around to the driver's side.

Gage was there holding that door for her, too. "I put the bag with the sandwiches and the condoms in the back seat."

"Thanks." She smiled at him. "I'll see that they get transferred to my room at the B&B."

"Then I guess we're all set." Nudging his hat back, he leaned down and gave her a quick kiss. "Let's get going."

The sensation of his lips on hers had been brief but potent. The next time she kissed him, they'd be alone in her room. But first she had to take him home and drive back to the B&B so Josh could have his nap.

Next would come the tough part, packing up Josh's things, transporting him to Wild Creek Ranch, and leaving without him. She was distracted as she climbed behind the wheel.

"I'm in. You can go."

"Right." She started the car and backed out of the parking space.

"When are you planning to take Josh to Wild Creek Ranch?"

"After he wakes up from his nap. He might take a long one after all this excitement. I talked with Kendra about it while you were riding around the pasture. I'm going to text her once he's awake."

He nodded. "Do you want me to come over there when you drop him off? Would that help?"

She smiled. "That's sweet, but I can do this. Once I'm back at the B&B, I'll text you."

"I'll be waiting."

19

Waiting was hell. Gage sat on the front porch with Pete and cleaned tack, which took up some time. During their conversation, he got around to telling Pete that he'd be spending the night with Emma at the B&B while their dad and Kendra kept Josh. Pete had already figured that one out.

"You know that's one of the reasons they're babysitting, so you two can be alone." Pete reached for a bridle draped over the porch railing.

"I suspected as much. Dad's in matchmaking mode for sure."

"How about you? I mean, more than the obvious. There has to be more to it than sex."

"That's what I intended to find out when I drove up to Great Falls on...damn, was it only last Thursday?" He hung up the bridle he'd been working on and took another.

"Time crawls when you're having a crisis."

Gage laughed. "Did you just make that up?"

"I did, as a matter of fact."

"Well, I like it. Might steal it." He rubbed saddle soap into the leather. "I know that technically this is a crisis, but I've had some really good times in the past couple of days. I don't think you're supposed to have fun during a crisis."

"Or maybe that's a sign that you've found someone special, someone who knows how to make lemonade out of lemons."

"Are you calling me a lemon?"

"This isn't about you, cowboy. It's about Emma, who finds herself in a difficult situation and manages to enjoy herself, anyway. Just in case you didn't notice."

"I did. She's been all in."

"Yet she'd never set foot in this town before and the only person she knew here was you. And you were a wild card."

"True."

"You know her better than I do, bro. But from what I've seen, you've stumbled upon a remarkable woman. Dad and Kendra think so, too."

"So they took Josh so I could seal the deal?"

"Oh, hell, no. Who knows if that's possible? Besides, I'm sure they couldn't wait to have that little guy to spoil. If that furthered the romance between you and Emma, bonus. I doubt they expected you to launch into any *sealing the deal* maneuvers."

"Good, because I'm miles away from that kind of thinking. Last Thursday I was investigating the possibility that Emma might turn into more than a two-week fling. Then things got real. My brain is nothing but scorched earth at this point."

Pete laid another bridle on the rail. "I'm guessing the rest of you is scorched for a different reason."

"Smartass."

"Just calling it like I see it. Nothing wrong with lusting after the mother of your child. I'd call that a definite positive."

"Theoretically. We were great together before, but it was all fun and games back then." He finished another bridle and hung it on the rail. "Neither of us had any responsibilities. It may not be the same."

"Maybe it'll be better."

That started his engines. "I'd better go shower and change." He stood. "I want to be ready when she texts me."

Pete laughed. "Something tells me you will be."

* * *

Gage parked in the visitor section in front of The Nesting Place and grabbed the bottle of red wine he'd picked up at the Guzzling Grizzly on his way through town. He'd tucked it into a GG wine bag from the Country Store. Flowers would have been nice, too, but they weren't available on a Sunday night.

Damn it, he was nervous. Yesterday he'd been over the moon about this opportunity. Earlier today he'd been trading sexual banter with Emma and looking forward to holding her. But like he'd told Pete, the dynamic wouldn't be the same as it had been nineteen months ago.

The front door of the B&B was still open at this hour and the entry was blissfully empty. He wasn't up to making small talk with Mrs. Stanislowski.

He'd settled the bill over the phone this morning before Emma had arrived with Josh. They wouldn't be coming back here next weekend because Kendra had invited them to stay at Wild Creek Ranch.

And yet, how would that work out? It didn't exactly set the stage for intimate encounters. Staying there would be great for his son, though.

He paused outside Emma's door, took a deep breath and focused on his purpose for being here. He'd promised to relieve her anxiety about Josh's first overnight with lots of hot sex. No pressure.

He tapped on the door and after a few seconds she opened it. Her mascara was smeared all to hell and she clutched a wad of tissues in one hand.

"Oh, Emma." Stepping inside, he set the bottle on the floor, nudged the door closed with his foot and wrapped her in his arms.

She clung to him and buried her face against his chest. "I'm...sorry." She gulped. "Silly. So silly."

"Shh, it's okay. Perfectly natural." He held her close and rocked her slowly back and forth. Lowering his head, he laid his cheek against her silky hair. She'd left it down. For him.

"I was fine." Her words were muffled against his chest. "Until I texted you."

"That made you cry?"

"No. The videos. I had the phone in my hand so I started watching them."

"Ah. Videos of Josh."

"Uh-huh." She took a shaky breath, lifted her head and gazed at him. "And now I look like some deranged chick from a horror movie."

He grinned. "Kinda."

"Hey! You're supposed to say I'm beautiful, no matter what."

He recited it in a monotone. "You're beautiful no matter what."

Her lips twitched. "Not like that. With feeling."

"You're bee-*you*-ta-ful, no matter *what!*" He lifted his eyebrows. "Better?"

She laughed. "Absolutely perfect. Makes me feel like a freaking goddess." She wiggled out of his arms. "If you'll excuse me, I'll go repair the— yikes! I got mascara all over your white shirt!"

He glanced down. "So you did."

"Take it off. Let me work on it right now before it sets."

Undoing his cuffs, he pulled out his shirttails and started on the row of snaps down the front. "Déjà vu all over again."

"Not quite." She stood back with her arms crossed. "This time I don't have to pretend I'm not looking. I can indulge in a full-out ogle."

"What's so great about a guy's chest, anyway? I never got that."

"Muscles. Women dig 'em. Pecs and abs. Yummy."

"Why?" He stripped off the shirt.

"Probably goes back to a time when a man needed brute strength to defend his family from the saber-toothed tiger. We're conditioned to be attracted to muscles."

"Sounds primitive."

Her eyes darkened and she moistened her lips. "Because it is."

"To hell with the shirt." Balling it up, he sent it sailing toward the table by the window. Then he took off his hat and scored a ringer on the bedpost behind her. "What, no argument about the stain on my shirt?"

She shook her head. "I like how this is going." Her breath came faster, now, rippling the dark green fabric of her top, loose-fitting with thin straps. No bra. The pants were made of the same stuff.

He unfastened his belt and slipped it out of the loops. "And I like what you're wearing."

"My PJs."

"Pretty slinky for PJs." He let the belt drop and unbuttoned his jeans as he walked toward her. "I don't remember those."

"I didn't wear PJs then." She swallowed. "I slept naked."

"I do remember that." He reached her and cupped her face in both hands. "Want to know what else I remember?"

Her pink lips parted as she sucked in a breath. "Sure."

"Your eagerness." He feathered a kiss over her soft mouth. "How you didn't even want to wait until I took my boots off." Heart racing, he touched down, tasting mint with the tip of his tongue, then hot desire as he slid deeper.

She moaned and gripped his shoulders, digging in with her fingertips the way she used to.

He cupped the back of her head and slipped a hand under the loose hem of her top. The pleasure of cradling the smooth, plump weight of her breast in his palm made him shiver. Slowly he stroked his thumb over her taut nipple.

Flexing her fingers, she began a firm, sensuous massage of his shoulders, then his pecs. When she pinched his nipples, he gasped and lifted his mouth from hers. "Emma..."

"I'm still eager, Gage." Her voice was low and sultry as she stroked his quivering abs. Then she moved lower, pulled down his zipper and slid both hands inside the elastic of his briefs.

A red haze of lust enveloped him as she grasped his cock in both hands. He groaned.

"Let's do it with your boots on," she murmured. "For old time's sake."

"Wonderful plan." He struggled to breathe. "Turn me loose so I can maneuver."

"All right." But she took her time about it, squeezing and fondling him before she finally let him go.

Scooping her up, he transported her to the bed and sat her on the edge. He had those flimsy pants off in two seconds, his jeans and briefs shoved down in another two. "Where are the—"

"Drawer." She pulled her top over her head and tossed it away.

He yanked the thing open and had to laugh. She had them scattered inside, loose and available. He snatched one up. "Handy."

"Told you I'm eager." She scooted a little farther onto the bed.

"Don't go too far away." He suited up. "I'm hobbled by these jeans, and...you know what? I should take the time to—"

"No. Come get me. It's tradition."

"Can't buck tradition." He crawled onto that bed the best he could, making sure his booted feet hung over the side. Easing between her warm thighs, he gazed into her green eyes as he sank his cock to the hilt.

Then he stayed there, not moving, not speaking, absorbed in the intense sensation of being with Emma like this. Again. At last. As if his body had been waiting.

She didn't move or speak, either, but a lot was going on with her judging from her expression. Aroused...happy...a little scared. Not so different from what was going on with him.

She *was* beautiful, no matter what. Smeared mascara and all.

Reaching up, she cupped his cheek. Her voice was soft and slightly breathless. "I wondered how it would be."

"Me, too."

"It's still good."

"Better."

Her smile reached right into his heart. "Yeah. Better."

20

What a miracle. Emma had never expected to see Gage again, let alone experience...*this.* They could have been awkward with each other. Tentative. Instead she lay beneath him dazed by the magic that had not disappeared. Instead it had grown stronger.

He held her gaze. "This is so perfect. I almost hate to move."

She smoothed her hands down his broad back. "But I love it when you do."

"I remember that." He rocked his hips, easing out and sliding back in. "You used to make noise."

"So did you." She sucked in a quick breath. That slight bit of friction had set off little explosions, hints of what would soon follow. "But that was winter, windows closed, my place."

"Don't worry." He drew back and pushed forward. "We'll manage this without bringing the house down."

"I'm not so sure." She clutched his hips and arched into his next thrust. "That feels really good."

"It's supposed to. Otherwise folks wouldn't bother." He continued the leisurely pace. "Ready to take it up a notch?"

"I could be persuaded."

"Mm, a challenge. I like that." Resting his weight on his forearm, he maintained the gentle rocking motion as he cupped her breast. "You used to like being touched here."

Her breath quickened. "Still do."

"I can tell." He began a slow massage. "You're squeezing my cock."

"And you like that." Everything was coming back, as if they'd parted days ago.

"Sure do. But I don't want to come. Not yet." He toyed with her nipple. "Ladies first."

"That's right. You never—"

"Point of honor. And it's time." Leaning down, he drew her nipple into his mouth.

The double assault of his sweet suction and the steady rhythm of his cock sent her flying over the edge. Her jubilant cry was cut short when he abandoned her breast and covered her mouth with his.

A moment later he lifted his head and gave her a chance to gasp for breath. "Noise level."

"I know." She gulped for air. "I forgot."

"Then I must have been doing something right."

"Quite a bit right. I was in outer space." Gradually she stopped quivering and peered up at him. "But you haven't—"

"No, but I will." He seated his cock more firmly inside her as his hot gaze roamed her body.

"I could almost come just looking at you, all pink and sweaty from your climax."

"I'm dripping. Did we sweat like this before?"

"Maybe not. It was winter."

"This is sort of erotic, getting all slippery."

"The earthy aspects of life."

"Yeah." She smiled. "Down to basics."

"Uh-huh, and speaking of that, remember how you used to wrap your legs around me?"

"Yes."

"I want you to do that. Tuck your heels against the small of my back. Open up for me."

"Here goes." She lifted her legs and crossed her ankles over his hips. "How's that?"

His chest heaved. "You can't imagine how great that feels."

"Probably not, since I don't have your equipment."

"No, you have complimentary equipment." Slipping his hands under her hips, he lifted her slightly. "This'll go fast, but I intend for you to—"

"Don't worry about me. Just go for it."

He smiled. "Does all this sound familiar?"

"Yes, yes, it does. Nothing changes, does it?"

"Oh, plenty of things have changed. Just not this particular discussion." He gazed at her. "You will come. You always do when I put the pedal to the metal. You like it fast and furious."

"I like it any way you dish it out, cowboy."

"I remember that, too." He began to move, slowly at first, then faster, holding her gaze as he ramped up the action. His heaving chest glistened and his voice was rough with passion. "Hang on."

She gulped for air as her quivering body began spiraling out of control. "I'm...with you."

"I know." His breathing grew ragged. "I can feel you tightening. So good..." He gasped and bore down. The bed began to shake. "Now, Em. *now.*"

Yes! She erupted, shoving her fist against her mouth to keep from yelling. Pleasure rolled through her, one glorious wave after another. Then he pushed home once more and shuddered, eyes squeezed shut, air hissing through his clenched teeth.

The pulse of his climax blended with the lazy undulations of hers as she gradually drifted down from that incredible high. His big body trembled. Throwing back his head, he took a deep breath.

When at last his gaze met hers, he took another long breath and lowered her hips to the bed. Then he began to smile, slowly, his dark eyes filling with happiness.

His smile triggered hers. "Doesn't get any better than that."

His eyes sparkled with mischief. "In that case, maybe I should pack up and vamoose. Quit while I'm ahead."

"Can I reword my comment?"

"Please do."

"That was a good start." She unwrapped her legs from around his hips, but he remained tightly wedged between her thighs. "What's next?"

"I was thinking along the lines of something like this." Leaning down, he settled his mouth over hers. "Mm."

"Mm-mm." She tunneled her fingers through his damp hair and savored the sweetness of an unhurried post-climax kiss. No agenda other than the sensual delight of mouth-to-mouth communication.

With Gage, kissing was an end in itself. He could turn the sensual dance of lips and tongue into an art form, and she was the lucky recipient of his talents. They'd often topped off their lovemaking this way, a gentle wind-down after a boisterous interlude.

She drifted in a romantic haze as he made love to her mouth. Then gradually he changed the action from deep and stimulating to light and playful as he nibbled on her lower lip. "You taste better than a hot fudge sundae."

"That's saying something."

"I know." He lifted his head and gazed down at her. "Hungry?"

"Little bit."

"I am, too. I've worked up an appetite."

"You haven't had anything since that sundae?"

"Only your delicious kisses. How about you?"

"The same."

"I brought wine."

"I saw that. Fancy bag, too."

"Let's have some. And eat our sandwiches." He dropped a quick kiss on her mouth. "But first I need to take care of the little raincoat." He eased away from her and climbed off the bed. "I'd forgotten how undignified the last part is after we do this with my boots on. And FYI, it was a lot darker in your bedroom." He turned away from her and shuffled into the bathroom.

She smothered a laugh. "Thank you for granting my crazy request." Grabbing her PJ top, she pulled it over her head before sliding off the bed to search for the bottoms.

"Don't get me wrong," he called from the bathroom, talking over the sound of running water. "Totally worth it. It's not a bad tradition, just awkward at the end." His boots thumped to the floor. "I'm taking them off, though."

"You can take off anything you've a mind to."

"Gonna keep on my briefs and jeans for wine and sandwiches." He came back out as she was pulling on her pants. "I see you had a similar thought."

"Yep. And I'm going to duck into the bathroom and wipe off the mascara."

"I'm growing fond of those raccoon eyes."

"You're such a flatterer." She slipped past him and went into the bathroom. "Yikes. This is what you were looking at the whole time?" She got out some cream and a tissue. "How did you keep a straight face?"

"I wouldn't have cared if you'd painted your face purple." He leaned in the doorway. "You wanted me. That makes me one damned lucky guy. Besides, you really are beautiful no matter what."

She chuckled. "Thanks." Wiping the last of the mascara away, she tossed the tissue in the trash and smiled at him. "Let's have dinner."

"I'll get the wine." He walked over to the door and picked up the bottle. "It's kind of ironic that we never drank a beer together or shared a bottle of wine, since you were a bartender."

"That wasn't something I wanted after serving drinks all night." She crossed to the kitchenette and picked up the shirt he'd tossed onto the table. At least it was white so it could probably handle bleach.

"And all I wanted was you." He pulled the wine bottle out of the bag. "I haven't tried this one but Michael says it's good."

"Is he a wine expert?" She tucked his shirt next to the coffee maker on the counter and took the sandwiches out of the compact refrigerator.

"Guess so. He's co-owner of the Guzzling Grizzly, so he needs to stay up on things like that. Got a wine opener?"

"I'm sure Mrs. Stanislowski would think of that." She opened a drawer. "Yep." She handed it to him before unwrapping the sandwiches and taking two plates out of the cupboard. "Michael's in the bar business?"

"The GG is way more than a bar. I'm fully behind this alternate dinner plan, but it means you don't get to see the GG. I'd almost say it's the heartbeat of the town."

"Really?" She put the sandwiches on the plates and carried them to the table along with a couple of napkins. "Must be a lot bigger deal than the little place where I worked."

"Well, the town is smaller than Great Falls and the bar is bigger than the one where we met, so yes, it's a big deal here. The Guzzling Grizzly is the only place in Eagles Nest where you can buy a drink."

"Cornered the market, did they?"

"I doubt it was intentional, but yeah. I can't imagine anyone competing with them." He pulled the cork from the bottle. "They have good food, live music and a dance floor, plus a Country Store that sells GG merchandise. Oh, and prints of my dad's scratchboard art is for sale there, too."

"Sounds like a happy place."

"It is." He opened a cupboard and took down a couple of glasses. "Sorry you're not there, instead?"

"Not on your life." She'd enjoyed admiring the play of muscles as he'd opened the wine. Might as well get the full benefit of his shirtless situation. She walked over and wound her arms around his neck. "If we were at the Guzzling Grizzly, I couldn't do this." Nestling against his broad chest, she gave him an open-mouthed kiss.

With a muffled groan, he slid an arm around her waist, set the bottle on the counter and drew her in his arms. *Mm.* Warm chest, strong arms, hot mouth.

The kiss quickly heated up. Cupping her bottom, he pulled her against the bulge in his jeans and lifted her off the floor in a move that was deliciously familiar.

She did her part by wrapping her legs around him as he carried her back to bed. This time he got rid of his jeans and briefs while she shimmied out of her PJs. They tossed back the covers for a change.

Tumbling onto the soft sheets, they rolled around on the bed, laughing and fondling each other with increasing urgency.

Finally, Gage reached over and opened the bedside table drawer. "Time to get serious."

"Can't. Having too much fun." She pinched his butt, which was temptingly on display.

"Hey." He shifted to face her. "Just for that, you get to open this and put it on."

"It won't fit. Not on my thumb, or my big toe, or my—"

"Put it on this, smarty-pants." He pointed to his very erect cock.

"Oh, *that.* It does look in need of being contained. It might 'splode any time now."

"No kidding."

She ripped open the package, tossed it away and rolled on the condom. "Happy, now?"

"I will be soon. One more thing." Moving to the end of the bed, he snatched his hat from the bedpost. "I'd count it as a personal favor if you'd put this on."

"On top of the condom?"

"On top of your head."

He'd remembered. That was special. "Now what?"

He stretched out on his back. "Climb aboard, please, ma'am."

She did as he'd asked, settling herself firmly on his rigid cock. "I guess we'll eat later."

"No worries." He grasped her hips. "The wine needs time to breathe."

_21_

Nineteen months ago, Gage had enjoyed a very good time with Emma. But not this good. She was funnier, sexier, and dear God, could she turn up the heat.

She had him begging for mercy before she finally gave herself—and him—the gift of a deeply satisfying mutual orgasm. And she'd done it all while wearing his black hat.

He hadn't been celibate for the past nineteen months, and naturally he'd worn that hat on dates. But he'd never suggested another woman put it on. Emma was the only one.

He staggered to the bathroom to ditch the condom and then returned to flop on the bed, still breathing as if he'd carried a football the length of the field. His hat was back on the bedpost and Emma lay beside him, as out of breath as he was.

Reaching for her hand, he interlaced their fingers and waited for his heartbeat to settle down. "Think we'll ever get to the sandwiches and wine?" He looked over at her.

"We need to if we plan to keep this up." She glanced at him and smiled. "Carbs would be helpful."

"Then let's make a plan. Once we have the energy to leave this bed, we'll climb out and eat the sandwiches to keep up our strength."

"And drink the wine. I'm glad you thought of bringing it."

"I got a kick out of Michael. He wanted to make sure you'd like it. He asked if you'd rather have red or white. I didn't know, but you seemed happy with the red Kendra served last night, so I—"

"Red is a great choice."

"Good."

Her brow puckered. "Then Michael knows you're spending the night with me?"

"Not specifically, but it's logical if I'm buying a bottle of wine to bring over here. That's kind of a tell, especially since everyone in the family's aware that my dad and Kendra are keeping Josh." He held her gaze, not sure if mentioning the baby would set off a reaction.

"Don't worry. I'm fine."

"You look fine. Calm."

"I am, now. Driving away from the ranch without him was very hard, though. If I hadn't done my makeup before going over there, I could have pulled off the road and had a good cry. Or come back here and cried it out. That would have been better."

He squeezed her hand. "You've never been through this. How could you know?"

"I do, now. First day of kindergarten, no eye makeup. Sunglasses."

First day of kindergarten. What a sobering concept. Did she want him to be there? Did he want to be?

"Anyway, the potential for ruining my makeup turned into a straitjacket. I couldn't cry so I convinced myself I didn't need to. But after I texted you I got nervous about how tonight would go. I thought looking at videos would be a good distraction."

"I'll bet that part worked like a charm."

"Sure did. I was too busy crying to worry about whether sex with you would be awkward after all this time."

He smiled. "Which it wasn't, at least not until I hobbled into the bathroom."

"I don't remember it being that funny before."

"Like I said, your bedroom was darker and the distance to your bathroom was only about four feet. Here it's more like eight or nine."

"I don't think you shoved your jeans and briefs down to your ankles the other times, either."

"Sure I did."

"No, I'm pretty sure you only pushed them far enough so you could put on the condom. I remember your jeans rubbing against my thighs and feeling the rough texture of the denim."

"The rough texture you're remembering was more likely my beard. Some nights I didn't have a chance to shave before coming over to the bar to meet you. Then if I—"

"No, that was different." Her eyes darkened. "I know what your beard feels like on my...thighs."

"Shouldn't be a problem tonight. I shaved right before I left the house." And he had a very strong urge to engage in that activity. He had some vivid memories of making her come that way.

Her breathing changed. "We said we'd eat our dinner."

"I have a different taste treat in mind." He lifted her hand and began nibbling on her fingertips.

"You're very good at this seduction business." Her voice was husky. "So before I completely lose my mind, I'm going to request a raincheck on that very tempting suggestion."

He stopped nibbling and met her gaze.

She took a deep breath, which made her breasts quiver invitingly. "Sharing our private little meal will be special, too."

He was touched that she was looking forward to it. Still aroused as hell, but touched. "You're right. Let's get dressed." Leaning over, he gave her a quick kiss. "If I eat everything on my plate, can I have dessert?"

She grabbed his head and pulled him down for a hot, wet kiss. Then she let him go. "Yes. You are without a doubt the sexiest man I've ever known."

"Thank you, ma'am." He grinned at her as he climbed out of bed and reached for his clothes. "You're the sexiest woman I've ever known."

"Then that works out very nicely for both of us."

As he was buttoning and zipping his jeans, he noticed an antique desk tucked into a cubby just big enough for it. He'd been so involved in Josh when he was here before, and Emma tonight, that he'd missed it entirely. A laptop sat on top of it.

He turned just as she finished putting on her slinky PJs. "Did you do some work today?"

"I did, while Josh was napping. That's prime time to get stuff done."

"What kinds of things do you do for your clients?"

"It varies." She walked with him over to the kitchen. "It's geared to individuals and small business owners. My most popular service is creating a robust online presence for those who don't have the time or expertise to make that happen."

"How do you do that?"

"I help them get out a newsletter, guide them through social media, teach them about online ads and write ad copy if they need me to, that kind of stuff."

He leaned against the kitchen counter and gazed at her. "Where did you learn to do that?"

"Taught myself some of it, found online resources for the rest. I'm still improving my skills, but these days you can learn almost anything if you have access to a computer."

"Might not be able to learn to ride a horse that way."

"That's true, but you could get some pointers and watch a few videos so you wouldn't go into it blind."

He nodded. "I'll grant you that. And teaching yourself enough to start a new business—that's impressive, Emma."

"Thank you."

"I know a few people in Eagles Nest who might want to hire you, my dad being one. Thanks to Roxanne he has a website, but I doubt he sends out a newsletter or spends much time on social media."

"I'd love to help him. Maybe when I come down next weekend I can talk to him about it. I'll text you the URL for my website and you can show him that, see if he's interested."

"I will. Ready to eat?"

"You bet." She glanced at the food sitting on the table. "I wasn't paying much attention when I unwrapped these sandwiches, but they're huge. Which is a good thing because I really am hungry."

"And thirsty?" He picked up the wine from the counter and grabbed the two stemmed glasses he'd found earlier.

"For wine and water. I'll get us some ice water if that sounds good."

"Yes, please." He poured the wine while she brought over two large water glasses and put those down at each place. "I noticed you lowered the blinds on the window."

"I thought it was a good idea, considering. Want to put it up now that we're semi-dressed?"

"Nope. I prefer the privacy." He pulled out a chair for her. "I don't know where you intended to sit, but this one has a view of the bed. That way you can contemplate our future activities while you eat."

"That's all well and good." She slid into the chair. "But that gives you a view of the sink."

"What sink?" He took the chair opposite her. "I don't see any sink. I just see you."

"You do have a way with words, Gage Sawyer."

"Thank you, ma'am. I'd rather have my way with you."

She laughed. "I think you have, cowboy. Twice."

"And we're just getting started."

"You might want to pace yourself. We've never had an entire night together."

"Let's toast that." He picked up his wine glass. "To spending an entire night enjoying each other."

"I'll drink to that." She touched her glass to his and drank. "And one more toast. To Quinn and Kendra, who made it possible."

"I'll definitely drink to them." He took another swallow. "Good wine."

"Very good. To Michael, who knows his wine."

"Hear, hear." He tapped his glass to hers and drank. "And to you, for being brave enough to bring Josh to Eagles Nest so I could have a chance to know my son."

"I'm so glad I did." She gazed at him over the rim of her glass. "And to you, for opening your heart to him."

"That I have." He raised his glass. "To us, for bringing such an awesome kid into this world."

She lifted her glass, too. "And to Josh."

"To our little family." He held her gaze as he touched his glass to hers and drank. She didn't repeat the toast, but she took a sip of her drink, which was kind of the same thing. He was starting to think of them as a family. Hard not to.

She put down her wine glass and gingerly picked up half of her sandwich. Pieces of lettuce, tomato and cheese tumbled out. "This will be a challenge."

"I'm sure you're up to it." He scooped his hand under his sandwich.

"I'm sure I am, but it's an advantage having big hands."

"Not when you're trying to thread a needle."

"You sew?"

"I struggle with it, like when a button pops off. Takes me forever, but it's either that or ditch the shirt."

"I like knowing that you sew buttons back on. I wouldn't have thought you'd bother."

He chewed and swallowed a bite of his sandwich. "We could probably fill a book with what we don't know about each other."

"Not the usual situation for the parents of a child."

"No, ma'am. But we can work on it."

"Could take a while. But we have tonight as a start. What do you think your dad and Kendra had in mind when they suggested it? I know they wanted to keep Josh, but—"

"I think they also did it to give us a chance to spend time alone, see what the dynamic is when Josh isn't here."

"It's a good idea."

He grinned. "Awesome idea."

"And not just because of that."

"I know. Couldn't resist. But it is nice to have a chance to talk about stuff, like your work, which I had no clue about. It's cool the way you switched gears. Do you like it?"

"Even more than I expected. I set my own hours and I can grow the business as I have more time to devote to it. Bartending had no future unless I wanted to own a bar, which I don't."

"I can see the appeal of being self-employed. Roxanne and Wes seem to like it. Guess I always wanted the security of that paycheck."

"Then you must feel really secure right now if you decided to take time off."

"I am, but it's starting to gnaw on me a little that money's going out and nothing's coming in except for the investments. I'll probably go job-hunting soon." He finished off his wine and picked up the bottle. "Can I top off your glass?"

"Sure. Thanks. What will you be looking for?"

He refilled their glasses. "Ranch work, most likely. I like the satisfaction of putting in a day of hard physical labor. I've about run out of projects at Dad's place. But I don't want to just get a job. I want it to be part of a plan."

"What kind of plan?"

He gazed at her. "It's still in the formulating stage."

"I see."

She probably did. He wasn't known for making firm plans or commitments so this was new territory for him. He couldn't claim to be adept at it.

But she had to suspect she and Josh were factors in whatever vague concepts he'd come up with. And how did she view his sudden appearance in her life? Did she even want a guy around? Had she dated?

That last question was nosy, but, what the hell. "You don't have to answer this, but your life seems to revolve around Josh. Have you dated at all?"

"No."

A knot of tension loosened in his gut. "Why not?"

"It's way too complicated a concept for me right now. I don't want to waste my time with somebody unless they're totally on board with the idea of Josh. Which means I have to like them, Josh has to like them—"

"Doesn't he like everybody?"

"More or less, which leaves me with the giant responsibility of figuring out if someone sincerely adores my kid or is faking it to make a good impression on me."

"But you're good at reading people. I've watched you at the bar. You'd have a guy pegged in seconds."

"Thank you. I'd like to think I'd know, but the stakes are so high now that I have Josh. It's easier to table my social life than take a chance."

"I can understand that."

She gazed at him. "You're looking extremely pleased."

"This is a delicious sandwich and really good wine. The company is outstanding. With all that going on, what kind of sourpuss wouldn't look pleased?"

"Admit it, Gage. You're happy I haven't dated anyone. Although I'll bet you have."

"I have, but I didn't—well, never mind. Yes, I'm happy that you haven't dated, which is not very evolved of me. You have every right to date. I should want you to find someone who's wonderful in bed and crazy about you and Josh."

"Yes, you should." She regarded him with a smile on those sweet lips.

"You know, it's the funniest thing, but when I drove up to Great Falls last week, it never crossed my mind that you'd have somebody else."

She blinked, but then she started laughing. "You do realize how arrogant that is, right?"

"Well, I suppose that's one way of—"

"You assumed I couldn't possibly be satisfied with another man after I'd been with the amazing Gage Sawyer."

"Yeah, that's extremely arrogant. I'm not proud of thinking that way. It's a failing." He grinned. "But is it true?"

"None of your business."

<u>22</u>

Emma hadn't admitted to herself that Gage had made an indelible impression, so she wasn't about to admit it to him. Didn't matter. He was sitting across the table with a cat-who-ate-the-cream expression on his handsome face. After her enthusiastic lovemaking, how could he doubt that she was wildly attracted to him...still?

She sighed. "Okay. It seems I have a weakness for you, Mr. Sawyer."

His gaze softened. "No more than I have for you, Ms. Green." He reached across the table and took her hand. "No one holds a candle to you, Emma. No one."

Now there was a comment to warm her all over.

"Why do you suppose I drove up to Great Falls to see you?" He caressed the back of her hand with his thumb.

"Guys look up old girlfriends all the time."

"I don't."

"That's hard to believe. Surely you—"

"No, I really don't. I figure what's done is done. But I couldn't forget you. I had this nagging feeling that leaving you had been a big mistake.

I've never had such a thought about a woman before."

Her heart beat faster. Quite a revelation from a man with Gage's history. "So you were just curious to see if the spark was still there?"

"It was a little more than that. I..." He glanced at their empty plates and wine glasses. "Looks like dinner is over. Could we continue this discussion in the comfort of that king-sized bed?"

"You want to get in bed and talk?"

"We used to do it all the time."

"I guess we did."

"We had a great conversation while we sat in bed drinking hot cocoa that one night."

"About what?"

"You don't remember?"

"Um...maybe something about wagon trains."

"Yep. Space ships as the Conestoga wagons of the future. Ordinary people leaving the world they know for a place they don't."

"Okay. It's coming back to me." She sent him a teasing glance. "Mostly I remember finishing the cocoa and fooling around with the can of whipped cream."

"Because you're a sexy wench." He stood and drew her out of her chair. "I figured that out the first night I came into the bar."

"You did not." Heat swirled low in her belly.

"I did so." Wrapping an arm around her waist, he tucked her against his hip as he walked toward the bed. "You looked up and smiled at me."

"I did that with all my customers."

"Ah, but then you focused on my mouth, long enough that I noticed and gave you a wink. Remember that?"

"Yes." *Vividly.* Moisture dampened her thighs. "You have a very sensuous mouth."

"Exactly what you told me the first night we spent together." He paused beside the bed, pulled her top over her head and tossed it away. "I asked what I could do for you, and you said—"

"Kiss me all over." The words came out on a sigh of anticipation. "That night was..."

"Magic." He pushed her hair away from her neck and nuzzled her there. "You're delicious. Every luscious inch."

The touch of his mouth drove her crazy. It had from that first night. She moaned softly. "Kiss me all over, Gage."

"Yes, ma'am. Be delighted to." His breath was warm against her throat as he slipped both hands beneath the elastic of her pants and tugged. They fell noiselessly to the floor.

Lifting her to the bed, he stood back to strip off his briefs and jeans. He was fully, powerfully erect. His hot glance roamed her body as she stretched out on the rumpled sheets. "Best dessert in the world."

She lay eager and quivering as his knee dented the mattress and he moved over her. Leaning down, he pressed his lips to her forehead. Then he lifted his head and gazed down at her. "You're shaking."

"Uh-huh. Excited."

"So am I." His voice was husky. "What an incredible night."

She sucked in a breath. "Yeah."

Lowering his head, he brushed his mouth lazily over hers. "Well, hang on, sweet lady. 'Cause I'm about to make that a *hell, yeah.*"

He moved from her mouth to the hollow of her throat with that same feathery touch, then over to her shoulder and down her arm. Slowly he made his way back to her other shoulder, the light pressure traveling over her sensitive skin like the stroke of butterfly wings.

She shivered with delight as he traced the slope of her breast, circled the underside and blew gently on her rigid nipple. Tension coiled within her as he continued his maddening, yet extremely erotic journey.

His warm breath and soft lips tickled and teased as he moved from her belly to her inner thighs. When he skimmed his mouth over her damp curls, she groaned. "You're killing me."

"Shh. I'm savoring." He grazed the backs of her knees on his way down to her toes and the bottoms of her feet. He made just enough contact to drive her insane.

She was panting by the time he returned, settled his mouth over hers and kissed her so thoroughly she almost came. Before she did, he drew back, breathing hard.

He swallowed. "Almost couldn't finish that routine. Damn, how I want you."

"I want you more."

His chuckle was thick with desire. "Doubt it."

"Then just..." She gasped for breath. "Just get a—"

"Not yet." He nibbled on her lower lip. "I'm still hungry." And he began a second, no-holds-barred trip down her body. This time he used his entire arsenal—licking, sucking and nipping until she was writhing on the bed.

Sliding between her thighs, he grasped her hips in his big hands. "Hold still."

"Can't."

"Never mind, then." He gripped her more firmly and pressed his mouth to her aching center.

That was all it took. Her climax roared through her and she arched upward. At the last second, she grabbed a pillow and screamed into it.

He held on, his tongue prolonging the ecstasy. As the shock waves ebbed, she sagged against the mattress, but he coaxed her back up to the summit. Wild with joy, she clutched her pillow and yelled some more.

He stayed with her until she stopped shaking. Then he gently lowered her to the bed. She lay sprawled beneath him, still holding the pillow over her face so she could moan and groan if she needed to. After a double climax lollapalooza, she might need to.

Moments later, he tugged lightly on the pillow.

She pushed it aside.

He was braced above her, his sheathed cock poised for action. His voice sounded strained. "Call me old-fashioned." He took a shaky breath. "But I need to see your face while I do this."

"Oh, Gage." Smiling, she stroked her hands down his sweaty back and grasped his hips. "I need to see yours, too. Come here, you crazy man."

He sank into her with a groan of relief. "Don't move for a minute. Let me...get control..."

"Don't know if I *can* move."

"Did I break you?"

"Just a temporary loss of power." She gazed into his warm brown eyes. "I'll regenerate."

"I predict you will." He pushed a little deeper. "Now that you're plugged in."

"You're a funny guy." But he was right. Now that his thick cock was firmly seated, her body was taking a definite interest in that fact.

"I know what I know. Your eyes tell me there's another climax lurking in that hot body of yours." He began to thrust.

"If there is, we might set a record."

"You kept track?"

"Only because I couldn't believe how many orgasms I was having every night with you."

He grinned.

"Don't get a swelled head."

"Too late." His breath came a little faster and he picked up the pace. "What's your record?"

"Five."

"That record's toast." Planting his hands on either side of her shoulders, he pushed himself up, shifting the angle. Then he bore down.

She gasped. He'd found her launch button. After only a few swift strokes, she was gloriously airborne. He leaned down and kissed her just in time to muffle her cry of release. Then, with a low-pitched groan, he surrendered, his chest heaving as he trembled in the grip of his climax.

She lay in a dazed stupor, barely registering when he left the bed to take care of the condom. Then the light in the kitchen flicked off. A soft buzz indicated he'd pulled up the blinds.

He walked back to the bed and paused beside it. What a treat for the eye. "You'll be driving tomorrow. I was thinking we should get some sleep."

"Lovely idea."

"I put up the blinds. I like waking up to the light, but if you—"

"I like that, too."

"Then I might as well turn off this lamp. Need anything?"

She held out her arms. "Just you."

"I sure like the sound of that." He switched off the lamp, climbed in and gathered her close. "Did Kendra expect you at a certain time in the morning?"

"No. She told me not to rush. She's set it up that Zane, Cody and Faith will feed the horses, but—"

"You'll be eager to fetch Josh."

"I will. I asked Mrs. Stanislowski if she'd be willing to put breakfast outside my door, to speed things up. She's going to add an extra portion for you, which is only right since you've paid for everything."

"I always intended to. Just didn't expect it to turn out this way." He kissed her gently. "What a spectacular ending to this weekend."

She snuggled against him. "Hell, yeah."

* * *

Six orgasms and the warm security of being held in Gage's strong arms guaranteed a deep sleep. But Emma's eyes snapped open when light crept through the window by the kitchen. Soon she'd see her little munchkin again. She couldn't wait.

Gage stirred, opened his eyes and smiled. "Mornin', beautiful."

Happiness flooded through her. "Mornin', handsome."

"Excited about seeing Josh?"

"Yes."

"Then let's get to it. If you want to hop in the shower, I can check to see if breakfast is outside the door, yet."

"Thank you." She cupped his bristly cheeks and kissed him.

Tunneling his fingers through her hair, he held her head and deepened the kiss. Just as the situation started to get out of hand, he drew away and sucked in a breath. "That's enough of that. You need to go get that little guy."

"I do." She scrambled out of bed before she changed her mind. "I probably shouldn't have kissed you."

"Yes, you should." He got up, too, and reached for his clothes on the floor. "We should always kiss each other when we feel like it. We just need a little willpower this morning. I'm sure Josh will be just as excited to see you as you are to see him."

"He will." She ignored Gage's magnificent body as she scooted past him and into the bathroom.

After her shower, she came out of the bathroom wrapped in a towel. Gage was setting up their breakfast at the little kitchen table. He'd put on his wrinkled, mascara-stained shirt and had rolled back the sleeves to his elbows. He hadn't bothered to fasten the front snaps.

With his shirt hanging open and the stubble of a beard darkening his chin, he was the perfect morning-after guy. Nothing like having a gorgeously unkempt, half-dressed man arranging breakfast.

He glanced up. "Want to put on your clothes, first, or—"

"I'll put on my clothes." She had a robe, but wearing only that while eating breakfast with a man as sexy as Gage could sabotage their efforts to stay focused. "I'll make it fast." She gathered up what she needed and went back into the bathroom.

When she came out, she was calmer.

He glanced at her. "You look great."

"Thanks." She walked over and slid into the chair he held for her. "You're easy to have around, cowboy."

"Exactly what I wanted to talk to you about."

"Oh?"

"How would you feel about having me come up to visit for a night or two this week?" He poured their coffee.

"Visit?" Alarm bells went off. A sexy interlude at the B&B had been a fun fantasy, but he was talking about inserting himself into her everyday life. That was a big step.

It could play havoc with her careful routine, too. "I don't know, Gage. I'm very busy during the week, and having you around would make it tougher to get my work done."

"I could help you with Josh. Entertain him while you work."

"I suppose, but there's the issue of meals, and—"

"I'd handle meals. I can cook or pick up something. I wouldn't expect you to treat me like a guest. I just hate the idea of waiting until next weekend before I see you and Josh again."

Josh would probably enjoy having him there. And after Josh went to bed...well, might as well admit she'd enjoy that part. "Just so you know that I have a lot to do, and I'd like to get ahead because I'll be taking time off again next weekend."

"I understand completely. I'll do everything I can to be an asset and not a liability."

"Then I guess we can try it and see how it goes."

"When?"

"How about Tuesday? Then I'll have time to settle in."

"Tuesday would be great. Knowing I'll see you soon will make it easier to say goodbye to you this morning."

"Speaking of that, are you going to follow me over to the ranch when I pick up Josh?"

"I would have if we hadn't made this new plan, so I could see him once more before you take off. But it might be simpler for everyone if you go get him and head on home."

"That makes sense." She gave him a teasing grin. "And this way, I can give you a proper goodbye kiss."

He waggled his eyebrows. "I prefer the improper kind."

"I'll see what I can do."

After breakfast, she quickly packed and he carried her suitcase to the car. After stowing it in the back seat, he opened the driver's door. "This is it."

"What a weekend." She gazed into his eyes, shadowed by his black hat. "I feel like a different person from the one who drove down here on Friday."

"I know I'm a different person from the guy who was sitting with Wes in the bakery." He cupped her face. "Thank you, Emma."

"You're welcome." She slid her hands up his chest and inside his open shirt collar. "Your shirt is still a mess."

"No worries. I'll use bleach on it." He rubbed his thumb over her lower lip. "You didn't put on lipstick."

"It's in my purse. I'll put some on later."

"Later?"

"After I give you an improper kiss." Rising to her toes, she ducked under his hat and captured his irresistible mouth. What pleasure he'd given her with that mouth.

He welcomed the slide of her tongue with a groan. As she took the kiss deeper and nestled against his broad chest, his breathing quickened. Then she began to slowly and deliberately suck on his tongue.

He groaned again and backed her against the car, caging her in, pressing his aroused body against hers as he plundered her mouth. When he finally broke away and stepped back, he was gasping.

She was in the same condition. "How...was that?"

He choked out a laugh. "I think you know."

"See you Tuesday." Pulse racing, she got in the car before she changed her mind and kissed him again. Her hands shook as she fastened the seatbelt.

He gripped the edge of the doorframe. "Stay safe."

"You, too." She met his gaze. "'Bye, Gage."

"'Bye, Emma." He closed the door and stepped back.

As she drove away, she glanced in the rearview mirror. He was still there, watching her leave. His visit to Great Falls might be a mistake, but after that hot kiss, she was ready to take the risk.

_**23**_

During lunch at his dad's house on Monday, Gage got a report on Josh's overnight stay. Evidently it had gone very well. They'd kept the little guy so busy petting horses and feeding chickens that he hadn't had time to miss his mom.

He'd been excited to see her come through the door that morning, but he'd shown no evidence of separation anxiety. Good news for everyone involved.

His dad had acted pleased about the trip up to Great Falls and amused by the gifts Gage had spent the morning buying. For Josh, he'd found a plush pygmy owl, a baby cowboy hat, a kid-sized football, and a wooden barn with a hinged roof that lifted to reveal the wooden farm animals tucked inside.

He'd gotten Emma a white t-shirt for flag football, a bottle of the red wine they'd had Sunday night, and a big bag of premium bird seed. For both Emma and Josh, he'd bought a print of _Home, Sweet Home_ at the GG Country Store. When he'd pulled that out, his dad had immediately taken it back to the studio so he could sign, mat and frame it for them.

Early Tuesday afternoon, Gage loaded his gifts in the truck and texted Emma so she'd know when to expect him. At his request, she'd promised not to make dinner. He'd handle it when he got there.

The drive seemed to take freaking forever, but when he parked in front of her house and checked the time, he was early. Must have exceeded the speed limit by...a lot. Damn lucky he hadn't been pulled over.

After evaluating the big pile of stuff on the passenger side of his cab, he chose to carry in only his duffle, the wine, and the plush owl. He'd get the rest later.

The neighborhood was quiet—kids in school, folks at work. Emma's front walk looked recently swept. The porch, too. He started to ring the bell, changed his mind and reached up to tap on the door instead.

She opened it before he could. "He's asleep," she whispered as she stepped back to let him in. She was barefoot. Her stretchy, short-sleeved top and yoga pants defined every sexy curve.

His groin tightened and he would have kissed her but he had his hands full. He kept his voice down, too. "I thought you said nothing woke him up."

"It hardly ever does, but—" She glanced at the plush owl. "That's adorable. And you wore your white shirt."

"Wanted to show you how clean it is."

"Glad the mascara stain came out. Can I help you with something?"

"I brought wine. I didn't know if we'll have a chance to—"

"I'll take it. We'll see. You can set the owl on that little table. And your duffle...you know where the bedroom is. Why don't you take it in there and I'll put the wine in the kitchen?"

"Sure, okay." He wanted to kiss her but circumstances weren't lending themselves to that. He went down the hall and paused by her spare room, now Josh's room. The door was open just a crack, not enough to see in.

He walked as quietly as possible past the door and into her bedroom. She'd moved the bed to a different wall and changed the bedspread. Otherwise the room looked about the same.

Good memories in this room. Hot memories. He set his duffle on the floor and laid his hat on top of it.

"Can I get you something to drink? Are you hungry?"

He turned. She stood in the doorway looking so tempting. Yes, he was hungry. But he needed to resist that hunger. "You said nap time was primo for getting stuff done. Were you working when I got here?"

"Yes, but you've been on the road for several hours. I have beer and lemonade, or maybe you'd like some—"

"I promised not to interrupt your work. If you don't mind me rummaging in the kitchen, I can find myself something to drink."

"I don't mind."

He stepped closer. "I just...I'd like to kiss you hello."

Her gaze softened. "I'd like that, too."

"Then you can go back to work and I'll just...get some lemonade or something."

"Right."

"Right." Sliding his arms around her waist, he pulled her close. "You feel so good."

"You, too." She wound her arms around his neck.

"Thanks for letting me come up to see you." He lowered his head.

Her voice was a soft murmur. "I'm glad you're here."

He made contact. Ahhh.

She opened to him with a sound low in her throat almost like a cat's purr. Music to his ears. He delved into her luscious mouth with a groan of pleasure.

Cupping the back of his head, she tightened her grip and deepened the kiss. Her breathing changed.

With great effort, he drew back just enough to be able to speak. "Emma..."

Her breath was warm on his mouth. "Can a girl change her mind?"

"You're sure?"

"I want you, Gage."

"All I need to know." He lifted her up so she could wrap her legs around his hips. Then he dived in for another hot kiss, crossed to the bed, laid her on it and followed her down, his mouth never leaving hers.

She fumbled with his belt while he reached under her shirt and flicked open the front catch of her bra. He had to stop kissing her long enough to strip off her shirt, and while he was at it he pulled off her yoga pants and panties.

Her breasts quivered with her rapid breathing. "Take off your boots this time."

"That's for sure." He sat on the bed to do it and caught himself before dropping them on the floor. Laying them down, he stood and quickly got out of his shirt.

He had condoms in his duffle, but on impulse he'd shoved one in his pocket. Concentrating on efficiency, he took it out, removed both jeans and briefs, and rolled on that little raincoat.

Climbing into bed, he moved between her damp thighs. When he buried his cock in her heat, he let out a deep sigh. "At last."

She gazed up at him. "It's only been two days."

"Seemed like two weeks."

"I know."

He began loving her slowly, but then she tightened around him. He wouldn't be able to last. He wanted this too much, wanted her too much. Stroking faster, he felt the first undulation of her climax.

She gasped. "Gage, I'm—"

"Me, too." Two more firm thrusts and they both came, breathing hard.

She gulped, swallowing her cries. He clenched his jaw and held back his cries, too. His heartbeat pounded in his ears.

Reaching up, she touched his cheek. "He's awake."

"He is?"

"Listen. He's talking to himself."

He held his breath so he could hear better.

The voice drifting from the other bedroom was soft and breathy. "Ma-ma-ma-ma...da-da-pa-pa-ba-ba-ba...mmmma-ma." Then came the distinct sound of a raspberry.

Gage looked at her and grinned. "Let's get dressed and go get him."

"Okay."

Swooping down, he planted a quick kiss on her sweet mouth. "Epic welcome."

"Epic response."

Five minutes later, he walked with her into Josh's room. The little guy sat in his crib, talking to his bluebird. He glanced up and his eyes got big. Then he quickly motored over to the railing and pulled himself up. "Da-da!"

Gage managed to talk past the lump in his throat. "Hey, sport." Walking over, he lifted him out of the crib. "How's daddy's best boy?"

"Da-da." He patted Gage's cheeks and bounced in his arms.

"Good to see you, too, buddy." He glanced at Emma. "Not random."

Her gaze was warm. "Not anymore." She came over, arms outstretched. "I need to change him."

"I'll do it if you'll supervise."

"All right. The changing table's right there." She pointed to it.

He carried Josh over and laid him down. "Efficient setup."

"I did my research."

"I can see that." He followed her instructions and changed Josh's diaper with a minimum of fuss. If she hadn't issued a warning, his son would have peed all over him, but that minor disaster was avoided.

"Well done, cowboy. You're probably eager to give him that cute owl, now."

"That plus the rest of it." He lifted Josh off the table and started toward the door.

"The rest of it?" She followed him down the hall.

"I picked up a couple of other things."

"For his birthday?"

"I meant them to be for that, but I'll just give them to him now and get him something else for his birthday."

"Hm."

He laughed. "I'm allowed. I'm almost twelve months behind on the gift-giving. Besides, it's not *that* much."

"How many things?"

"Just a few." He walked into the living room, which also wasn't quite the same as he remembered, although he hadn't spent much time in that room when they'd been dating. The Green Bay pennant was still on the wall behind what looked like a new sofa and the Packers throw lay over the back of it. "Did you get a different sofa?"

"Same one. Had it recovered in a fabric that would resist stains."

"Smart." The computer desk hadn't been here before, though, and neither had a large wooden container with a hinged lid. "I'll bet that's his toy box."

"Yep. It's where I dump everything when he takes his nap. He'll want to start digging into it soon. In fact, you can put him down and let him roam."

He hoisted Josh up a little higher so they could look each other in the eye. "What do you say, buddy? Want to get down?"

"Da-da." The baby leaned forward and carefully pressed his wet little mouth on Gage's cheek.

He blinked. "Was that a kiss, squirt?" He looked over at Emma. "Did he just give me a kiss?"

"Yep. Kendra and Quinn taught him."

"That's so sweet." He turned toward Josh. "Now Daddy will give you a kiss." He placed a gentle one on the baby's soft cheek.

Josh crowed with delight, then started wiggling to get down.

"Okay, buddy, there you go." After he lowered the baby to the floor, he glanced at Emma. "Dad said the overnight worked out great."

"They were wonderful with him. I don't think he missed me much at all."

He smiled. "You okay with that?"

"I am. Clingy and dependent is not my style. I don't want it to be his, either. We all went out back to watch the chickens, and Josh is entranced with them. If my landlord would allow it, I'd get some."

"Would you have time to deal with chickens?"

"I could make the time. Kendra's busy, too, but she worked it into her schedule." She turned her attention to Josh, who'd crawled over to the toy box and pulled himself up. "It would be fun for me and great for Josh, but the landlord might not approve it and the zoning might not allow it."

"Something to check into." Except...a chicken coop and chickens would mean she couldn't get away for visits as easily. His plans were still hazy, but if he got a job he wouldn't be able to drive up here that often, either. And being with Emma and Josh was becoming a priority.

"Yeah, I will. Listen, before I open the toy box, why don't you give him the owl?"

"Okay." He walked over to the table beside the door and picked it up. "Let's see if it's a hit or a miss." Approaching Josh, he crouched beside him. "Brought you a little something, buddy." He held out the owl. "What do you think?"

Josh let out a soft little *oh* of surprise as he gazed at the owl. Then he reached out and touched it. "Ba-ba?"

"Yes, bird. Owl. Like we saw at Raptors Rise. They make a sound like this—*hoo, hoo-hoo.*"

Josh stared at him. Then he giggled.

"Like the way that sounds? *Hoo, hoo-hoo.*"

He giggled louder. "Ba-ba!" He grabbed the owl's head.

"It's yours if you want it." He slowly let go.

Grasping the edge of the toy box for support, Josh clutched the owl to his chest. His voice softened. "Ba-ba."

"All yours, buddy." First gift. The kid was so young. He wouldn't remember this moment. But Gage would never forget it.

24

Before dinner, Emma suggested they go for a walk. She could use a little fresh air to clear her head, and Gage was gung-ho to try out the baby carrier.

After he familiarized himself with the straps and buckles, he had Josh strapped on his back in no time. Josh was sitting several inches higher than when she took him, and he clearly loved the extra height, babbling away as they strolled through her neighborhood.

Gage chuckled. "It's like he's speaking a foreign language."

"I know. He has all the inflections right, but nothing makes sense."

"Do you think he's trying to say something, though?"

"Not according to what I've read. He's mimicking our speech patterns, but he doesn't have the tools to say words the way we do, or put them together in a sentence. But it's coming. I can't wait." She waved to a neighbor who'd just come home from work. Another neighbor drove by and lightly beeped the horn.

"Friendly place," Gage said.

"It's a good neighborhood, especially for children. I haven't had as much time to socialize since Josh was born, but I'm sure that will change as he gets older and he can play with the other kids."

"I hadn't thought about that. We didn't have close neighbors but I had my brothers and my sister. You had to be old enough to ride a horse before you could go to somebody's house to play."

"So different from the way I grew up. I probably chose this neighborhood because it feels familiar." She cautiously maneuvered through this conversational minefield about choices made, choices yet to be made. The future had become tougher to predict.

"You seemed to enjoy Wild Creek Ranch, though."

"Oh, I did. I can see the appeal of a place like that. Josh had a blast with the critters."

"Sounds like it from what my dad said. You can bet he and Kendra will be eager to get him a pony when he's old enough."

"And I'm sure he'd love it, although if he's only there every so often...no point in worrying about it yet, I guess."

"Right. Speaking of gifts, Dad wanted me to thank you for the list. Big help."

"It's going to be a mountain of presents, though, isn't it?"

"Yeah." He laughed. "I don't know how you can avoid it since Josh is the first baby in the family."

"I'm touched that they're all so eager to celebrate. It'll be fine if he gets too much. I'll just quietly put some of it away and bring things out one at a time, spaced out over the next few months."

"So maybe I should hold off on giving him the rest of what I brought."

"On the contrary. You're his daddy. Your gifts get top billing." And she was curious about what he'd chosen. "What did you get?"

"Will he understand what I'm saying if I tell you? I want them to be a surprise."

She grinned. "He *might* understand if he was listening, although he still wouldn't get the whole picture. But he's not paying any attention to us, so you can tell me."

"I'll keep my voice down, just in case. I got him a cowboy hat like the one he wore Sunday."

"Awesome."

"And I found a kid-sized football. It's even green and gold."

"Perfect. He'll love it."

"The other thing is a wooden barn, and you lift up the lid to get out the wooden animals. Lead-free paint and no small pieces. I mostly got it for the horse, but there's a cow, and a pig and—"

"Chickens?"

"Two, I think."

"Great idea. All the presents sound excellent."

"Nothing's wrapped."

"That's actually better. Maybe you could start with the barn tonight and we can all play with it. Then you can bring out the football and the hat tomorrow."

"Okay. I also got a large bag of bird seed."

"Ha! Thanks! You must be psychic because I'm running low."

"I am psychic. I just don't like to brag about it."

"Are you really? Then what are we having for dinner?"

He pressed a hand to his forehead. "Hang on, it's coming to me...homemade soup."

"You are such a poser. You saw the container I left on the counter to thaw."

"You're thawing homemade soup? Wow, what a coincidence."

"Give it up, Sawyer. I'm onto you."

"Yeah, but what's with the soup? You promised not to cook."

"I'm not cooking. I'm just heating some soup."

"Semantics."

"I wasn't in the mood for take-out and this is quick and easy. You can heat it up if that would make you happy. You can also fix the toasted cheese sandwiches."

"You must be psychic, too, because toasted cheese is my specialty."

"I am psychic, and I brag about it constantly." Teasing each other had been their pattern when they'd been dating. Nice to know they still could.

* * *

Josh had a great time eating his toasted cheese sandwich. He got melted cheese globs everywhere, including in his hair.

When Gage offered to clean him up, Emma gladly handed him a wet washcloth. Then she took Josh into the living room to wait while Gage went out to his truck to fetch the toy barn. His eagerness to buy gifts for his son was understandable. And heartwarming.

He came back with the wooden barn under one arm and two more flatter packages under the other. Those were wrapped, though, and he'd said Josh's weren't. Evidently she was getting presents, too.

He laid those two on the floor without comment and set the barn in front of Josh, who was currently holding both his bluebird and his owl. Josh gazed at the red barn with the green roof and then peered up at Gage.

"You want to know what the heck this is, don't you, sport? What kind of tomfoolery is Daddy up to, huh? I'll show you. This is a barn, and the roof comes off. Ta-da!"

Josh leaned forward, looked inside, and squealed. "Ba-ba!" Dropping both his bluebird and his owl, he reached in and pulled out a chicken. Then he tossed that down and brought out another one. "Ba-ba!"

Emma grinned. "I'm telling you. Chickens."

Sticking his hand into the barn again, Josh came up with the horse. He stared at it a long time.

"Horse," Gage said. "It sounds like this." And he whinnied.

Emma started giggling. "You do that so well."

"Naturally. When you're a kid on a ranch, you mimic all the animal sounds."

"I guess you would." She glanced at Josh. "Look at his eyes. He thinks you've lost your mind."

He smiled. "He wouldn't be the first to think that. Hey, buddy, can I borrow your horse for a minute?" He held out his hand.

Josh laid the horse right in it.

"Thank you for sharing. Here's one thing you can do with this horse. You can make him gallop along the floor, like this." He demonstrated. "And you can pretend he's rearing up." He whinnied again. "Want to try it?"

"Da-da!" Josh took the horse and scooted it along the floor making a funny little noise in his throat. Then he tipped the horse up and squealed.

"Perfect! You've got the idea."

"Oh, my God, I should be videoing this."

"I am," Gage murmured. "In my head."

Aww. He'd been earning points ever since he'd arrived, and the depth of caring in that soft-spoken comment earned him a whole bunch more.

Josh continued to pull animals out of the barn and Gage made the noises for each one. Once they were all out, Josh methodically put each one back in. Then he took them out again, making his version of the noises his daddy had taught him.

Emma smiled at Gage. "I think you have a winner."

"I was hoping." He picked up the top package from the two lying next to him. "This is for you."

She tore the white tissue paper where it was taped together and pulled out a white t-shirt. "Woo-hoo! I'll bet this is for football!"

Josh twisted around toward her, a chicken in each hand. "Ma-ma!"

"Look, Josh! Mommy has her own shirt for flag football." She held it against her chest. "Want to go watch Mommy and Daddy play football again?"

He waved the chickens in the air. "Ba-ba-ba-ba-ba!"

"And go see Granny Ken's chickens. You bet."

"Ba-ba." He returned to his task of emptying the barn and refilling it.

She glanced at Gage. "Thank you. It's funny, but I don't have a white t-shirt. I was thinking of buying one."

"Now you don't have to." He picked up the other package, which was the size of a large coffee-table book and about that heavy. It was wrapped in brown paper, the corners neatly folded and taped. "This is just...because."

She undid the tape and folded back the paper to reveal the back of a framed picture. When she turned it over, she gasped. "It's *Home, Sweet Home.*" She looked up and met his gaze. "I love this."

"I saw how you looked at the original. I got Dad to sign it. Then he insisted on matting and framing it."

"What a beautiful job he did." She looked more closely at the print, and sure enough, Quinn's signature was in the bottom corner. "This is so special. For me and for Josh. His grandfather's creation. He won't understand that for a few years, but eventually he will." She leaned toward him. "Thank you so much." She gave him a gentle kiss and drew back.

Warmth filled his dark eyes and a smile crinkled the corners. "I'm so glad you like it."

"*Love* it," she corrected. "Love. It. I know just where I want to put it, too." She scrambled to her feet. "I'll get a hammer."

"Josh and I will be right here playing with the animals."

As she came back from the laundry room with the hammer and the picture hook, clucking noises drifted from the living room. She paused at the end of the hallway.

Gage and Josh each had a chicken, and those birds were clearly having a conversation. Gage did most of the clucking, but Josh was catching on fast. They were bonding.

Gage looked up when she walked into the room. "Need some help?"

"Sure. I want it over my desk so I can see it all the time."

"It'll look great there." He glanced at Josh. "I need to take a break so I can help Mommy hang a picture, buddy. Would you please hold my chicken?"

"Kuk-kuk!"

"Thanks, sport. Good job." He stood and brought her the picture.

"You've increased his vocabulary."

He grinned. "You never know when being able to cluck like a chicken or moo like a cow will come in handy."

"Absolutely. Okay, I'd like the picture centered over the desk, and maybe about eighteen inches above it. If you'll hold it up, I'll eyeball it."

He surveyed the space, leaned over the desk and held the picture in place. During dinner, she'd been focused on the meal and Josh, but with Gage posed with his back to her, she was getting a great angle on his firm buns.

He edged sideways so she could see. "How's that?"

"Up a little. Now over to the left." The snug fit of those Wranglers was messing with her concentration. "Down a little... A bit more..." What was it about wear-softened denim? It was so—

"Em? Is that good?"

She snapped out of her daze. "Perfect. "If you'll just tip the bottom out a little, I can put my finger on the spot." She walked back to the desk.

"Like this?"

"Uh-huh." His gentle breathing and the warmth of his virile body made her shiver as she moved in closer and reached under the frame.

"When's his bedtime?" His murmured words slid over her like warm syrup.

"Pretty soon."

"Can I help tuck him in?"

"Sure." And after that, she could look forward to spending the rest of the night in his daddy's strong arms. What a lovely prospect.

25

Heaven was only minutes away. But Gage didn't want to rush Josh's bedtime routine. He hadn't been part of it until tonight.

After bath time with a flotilla of rubber duckies, Emma snapped the little guy into his soft cotton PJs decorated with bluebirds. Then she handed him to Gage and pulled out a picture book from a shelf in his bedroom. "This is his favorite. It's about the adventures of three friends who happen to be ducks."

He smiled. "Can't wait to hear it."

Josh insisted on holding both his bluebird and his owl during story time. Tucked between Gage and Emma on the sofa, he pointed at the pictures and babbled away as usual, only now he threw in *kuk-kuk* every so often.

Gradually his little body relaxed and his grip loosened on his precious birds. His comments trailed off. He yawned. By the time Emma closed the book, his eyelids were drooping.

"Can I put him to bed?"

Her voice was muted. "Of course."

Getting slowly to his feet so as not to jostle the baby, Gage gently scooped him into his arms and laid him against his chest. Like that first time in Wes's apartment, Josh melted into him in a gesture of complete trust.

Emma led the way into the room lit only by the glow of a night-light. He laid the baby in his crib and Emma tucked the birds in beside him.

Josh's eyelashes fluttered. "Ma-ma."

"Sweet dreams." She leaned over and kissed his cheek.

"Sleep tight, buddy." Gage kissed him, too.

Emma quietly raised the railing until it clicked into place. Then she slipped her hand into Gage's and laced her fingers through his.

He tightened his grip. His need for her simmered, adding depth to a moment so rich with emotion that his throat hurt. This precious child was the result of having lusty, glorious sex with the woman by his side. That hadn't quite sunk in until now.

He'd been overwhelmed by Josh's sudden appearance, then steamrolled by the pressure of events that had followed. But in the peaceful quiet of his son's bedroom, the soft sound of Emma's breathing made him ache with a visceral craving that nearly overpowered him.

She squeezed his hand and he glanced down. She mouthed the words *let's go* and started for the door.

And oh, he was ready. Once he was in her bedroom, he tugged her close, his voice hoarse with urgency. "I'd planned to take it slow, but if I'm not deep inside you real soon, I might go crazy." He drew in a ragged breath. "I want...I *need...*"

"I know." She looked up at him, her green eyes luminous. "I need you, too."

With a groan, he captured her mouth. He poured every bit of his longing into that kiss until they were both trembling. Then he undressed her quickly and lifted her onto the bed. Holding her gaze, he took off his clothes. The job was tougher than usual because he was so eager.

By the time he put on the condom and climbed into bed, he was truly shaking, desperate to make that essential connection with her. He slid in, absorbing the intense pleasure of that sweet friction, her moan of pleasure, the way her eyes darkened and her cheeks flushed.

Her fingertips pressed into the muscles of his back and she arched upward in a silent invitation to go deeper. How he loved that. Burying himself to the hilt, he held his breath until the urge to come passed.

She tightened around his cock. A hitch in her breathing told him all he needed to know. He didn't have to move much. Easy does it. Just a little rocking motion and...right there. *Ah, Emma.*

Leaning down, he covered her mouth with his and muffled her first cry of release. Then he lifted his head to let her gulp in air and timed his slow strokes to the waves of her climax. *Don't come, don't come, don't come.* Somehow he held back as she bucked and gasped beneath him.

Panting, she sank to the mattress and closed her eyes. "So...good."

"For me, too." Anchored in tight, he rode out the aftershocks.

Her eyes slowly opened. "But you—"

"I love watching you climax."

"Oh." She took a shaky breath.

"And feeling it." He began to pump. "I'll bet you'd like a repeat."

She smiled. "Smart guy." She slid both hands to his butt and began a slow massage.

Nice. But it made him want to...oh, yeah, sure did.

"I like it when you come, too." Her warm gaze locked with his. "When we come together. That's special."

The emotion in her eyes opened the floodgates. *Emma.* Fierce longing gripped him. And he was undone. Powerless to hold back...anything. He surrendered to a driving need to thrust into her over and over until her cries mingled with his.

Braced above her and breathing hard, he tried to get his bearings. He'd never let go like that. Never. He swallowed. "That was..."

She cupped his face in both hands and took a deep breath. "The best ever."

"Yes." More than that. He didn't have the words, yet. Just a conviction that his world had shifted. "Good thing we didn't wake him up."

"Like I said, he's a sound sleeper." She smiled. "Kind of like old times, huh?"

He couldn't stop looking at her. Her taffy-colored hair was tangled every which way and her skin was rosy from making love...with him. God, she was beautiful. "Better than old times." He sucked in another breath. "Way better."

* * *

Because the night was still young and there was ice cream in the freezer, Emma suggested they each get a bowl to take back to bed. That turned into some fun fooling around and another mutual orgasm before they packed it in.

Gage woke up the next morning to the aroma of coffee, the sound of Josh babbling, and Emma's side of the bed empty. Pulling on his briefs and jeans, he went into the kitchen, where she was feeding Josh warm cereal. Her hair was damp.

"Morning, beautiful."

She glanced up and smiled. "Morning, handsome."

"Da-da!"

"Morning to you, too, sport." He glanced at Emma. "Did I sleep through you taking a shower?"

"Yep."

"I must be feeling really relaxed to do that."

"You look really relaxed."

"And in need of a shave and a shower. If you can wait until after I do that, I'll make breakfast."

"Sure thing. Want coffee?"

"As soon as I get back out here. I won't be long." He stripped off his clothes in the bedroom and walked into the bathroom, fragrant with scents he associated with her.

The basket of tub toys made him smile. How cool to have been part of that routine last night. The kid did love his bath.

He shaved quickly at the sink before taking a shower. An idea had come to him soon after waking up and it wouldn't leave him alone. Was it doable? Would she go for it? Only one way to find out.

Toweling off, he dressed in the clean clothes he'd packed into his duffle. He'd worn the white Western shirt to show her the mascara was gone, but he pulled on a t-shirt this morning. Seemed more practical for a day spent playing with Josh.

He walked back into the kitchen as she was lifting the little guy out of his high chair. She glanced over at him. "Before we start our breakfast, we need to feed the birds."

"Right! Are you okay on seed? Because I can go get the bag from the truck."

"I have enough to fill it this time. Maybe today while I'm working you can take Josh outside and put the seed in my little can."

"Will do. Want me to take him, now?"

"I think he'd like that. Ready to go see Daddy, Josh?"

He reached for Gage. "Da-da-da-da-*kuk-kuk*."

"Cluck-cluck to you, too, squirt." He swung him into his arms. "Which way, Emma? Is there a back door?"

"Follow me." She had on her running shoes this morning and the rubber soles squeaked on the wooden floor as she hurried through the laundry room to the back door.

The birds were waiting. They fluttered and chirped in the branches of an oak tree in the yard. Emma had hung a baby swing from one of the branches. A little sandbox sat on the ground nearby.

"You've done an amazing job setting up this place for him."

"It was fun." She opened the lid of a small trashcan. "Birdseed's in here. Eventually he'll be big enough to scoop it out and fill the feeder, but we're not quite there, yet. If you'll take him to it, I'll bring the seed."

"Got it." He located the bird feeder, a little house-like structure on a pole. His mom's feeder had been similar. He'd kept it filled until he'd left home. "Hey, buddy, these birds sound hungry. Should we give them breakfast?"

Josh swiveled back and forth, trying to keep track of the chattering birds swooping in and out of the branches of the oak tree. "Ba-ba! Kuk-kuk-kuk!"

"I'll take that as a yes. Josh thinks these birds need food, Emma."

She approached with a scoop of birdseed, lifted the hinged lid on the feeder, and poured it in.

Josh chortled with glee.

"Now we retreat towards the house and wait for them to gather." She walked backward away from the feeder. "Josh loves this part."

He'd loved that part, too. He had a catch in his throat as the birds flocked to the little house and Josh quivered with excitement. "This is great, Emma. I'm so glad you put this here for him."

"With the way he reacts to them, I couldn't imagine not doing it."

"Because you're a good mom."

"Well, thank you for that." She stood there a little longer before turning toward Josh. "Let's get you set up by your window, okay?"

"Ba-ba."

Gage followed her inside, where she positioned his highchair by a window with a good view of the activity. "I'm guessing you planned that feeder's location."

"You know it. I love my son, but I'm not prepared to stand out there for two hours while he watches the birds eat."

"Would he last that long?" He settled Josh in the highchair.

"Maybe not, but I don't want to chance it." She poured some Cheerios on his tray. "Dinner and a show." She turned to Gage. "Our turn."

"I'm on it. Eggs? Bacon? Toast?"

"Check, check, check."

"Then hand me the stuff and turn me loose."

"But I'd be glad to—"

"Nope, nope. Just stick around and keep me company."

"I'm not letting word get out about this, cowboy. A man who looks like you and can also cook? The women will be lining up." She hauled out the pans he'd need and took a carton of eggs and a package of bacon out of the fridge.

"Yeah, please keep it quiet." He melted butter in a pan. "I have my hands full with you."

She leaned against the counter. "That better be a compliment."

"Oh, it is." He gave her a wink. "I'm a lucky man and I know it. How do you like your eggs?"

"Over easy, but not overdone. I like the yolk to have some give to it."

"How about your bacon?" He peeled off several strips, laid them in a second pan and turned on the heat.

"Crisp but not brittle."

"Challenge accepted." He plugged in the toaster and loaded it with slices of bread.

"You've done this a time or two."

"Dad taught us to cook. Pete and I embraced the concept. I'm not sure that Wes and Roxanne ever did. But Roxanne's marrying a man who co-owns a restaurant and Wes is in love with a baker. Since preparing food isn't a high priority for either of them, they chose wisely."

"Sounds like it."

He cracked the eggs in the pan two at a time because...might as well admit it...he was a bit of a show-off when he was good at something. "I have an idea I'd like to throw out to you."

"Should I suit up? Get a catcher's mitt and a face mask?"

"No, ma'am. I'm just lobbing this one in, hoping it looks decent enough that you'll consider going for it."

"What is it? I'm on pins and needles."

"You and Josh moving to Eagles Nest." He glanced over to gauge her reaction and blinked.

They'd had a great weekend and yesterday had been a huge success. The three of them got along better than he could ever have predicted. But she had to realize that the physical distance between them was a problem, one a move to Eagles Nest would solve.

He'd anticipated hesitation, maybe some anxiety, possibly even a tiny bit of excitement. Questions, of course. They'd have a lot to discuss regarding this possibility.

But he hadn't prepared himself for shocked silence. The frozen expression on her face was unsettling.

"So." He cleared his throat, his hope fading. "Guess that doesn't sound good to you."

"No, Gage, it doesn't. In fact, it sounds like the worst idea in the world."

26

Gage looked as if she'd slapped him. Emotionally speaking, she probably had. But what the hell was he thinking? She took a quick breath. "Let me rephrase that."

He eyed her warily. "Okay."

"Your suggestion seems very spur-of-the-moment. How long have you been considering this?"

"I suppose it's been in the back of my mind since the weekend, but the three of us have been getting along so well that it seemed natural to bring it up this morning."

"You haven't even been here a full day."

"I know, but don't you agree we get along great?"

"So far! But what happens when life isn't this smooth?"

"Why wouldn't it be?"

She blinked. Oh, yeah. He didn't know much about babies. Or relationships. "Josh isn't always this easy. He's fussy when he's teething. Sometimes he gets sick and is up all night with a fever. Or a tummy ache, or an earache, or—"

"But you wouldn't have to deal with all that alone anymore. In fact, it's a perfect reason to move down to Eagles Nest. You'd have all kinds of help with Josh."

That nicked her pride. "I've been managing very well on my own. I have my support system in place. Josh is used to this house and our routine. We like it here. I'm not going to uproot him—or me—on a whim."

He scrubbed a hand through his hair. "It's not a whim. And think of all you'd gain! Maybe I jumped the gun suggesting it right now, but it would be great. We'd work out all the details as we went along."

His earnestness was endearing, if misguided. "Your saying that tells me you haven't thought this through. You've asked me to move to Eagles Nest with Josh, but can you guarantee that you're planning to stay?"

"Of course I'm staying. My entire family's there."

"When I met you, your entire family was in Washington State, but you were living in Montana."

"True, but I knew I didn't want to stay in Washington. Eagles Nest appeals to me and I can tell it appeals to you, too."

"It does appeal to me, but so does Great Falls. And you haven't exactly put down roots, yourself. How invested are you in that town?"

"I'm working on it. And think how beneficial it would be for Josh, living close to my dad and Kendra."

And look at how nimbly he'd dodged her question. "He'd love seeing them, but here he has playmates next door and a school right down the street. He can live in this house and visit his grandparents regularly. It's not that far."

"Far enough." He frowned. "And what about us?"

She gazed at him in frustration. He was giving her all questions and no answers. "What *about* us?"

"We're four hours apart!"

"I know that."

"And that doesn't bother you?"

"It might not be ideal, but—" The acrid odor of burned bacon and eggs filled the kitchen.

"Damn." He turned around and surveyed the smoking pans. "So much for breakfast."

That was the least of their problems. "It's fine. We can start over."

He sighed. "No, we can't." He shut off the burners and faced her again, his gaze flat, defeat and resignation in the slump of his shoulders. "Look, this discussion is going nowhere. Maybe it's best if I get my stuff and take off."

She swallowed. That sounded like the Gage she knew. The one who'd walked out her door a year and a half ago. "Are you sure?"

"Yeah. It'll give us both time to think." He dumped the burned food in the garbage and ran water in the pans before leaving the room.

She stayed where she was. *Breathe.* In, out, in, out. He couldn't see the issues. Or he refused to. Either way, the ball was in his court.

Duffle in one hand, hat in the other, he came back into the kitchen, walked over to the highchair and crouched next to it. "Gotta go, buddy. You be a good boy for your mama, okay?"

"Da-da!" Josh held up his arms and bounced in his seat in a clear bid to be picked up.

"Sorry, sport." His voice cracked. He gave Josh a quick kiss on the cheek and stood. He held her gaze. "Sorry, Emma." Cramming his hat on, he walked out of the kitchen. The front door opened and closed.

When the truck didn't start right away, her stomach churned. Was he rethinking their discussion? Coming to a different conclusion?

And if he didn't...this fun interlude was over. Really over. But he was Josh's daddy. Which meant he could be in her life forever. And if he couldn't understand why she wasn't willing to give up everything she had to take a chance on his vague promise, their future would be no fun at all.

Something thumped on the porch. What the heck? Walking quickly through the living room, she opened the front door just as he put the truck in gear and drove away.

She gazed at the items he'd left—a bag of seed, a small football, and a baby cowboy hat. When the image blurred, she closed the door.

* * *

Gage didn't remember driving home, but somehow he got there. His dad's truck was gone. Since it was past noon and his dad's studio time was officially over for the day, he could be anywhere—in town, over at Kendra's, in Bozeman picking up a part for his Harley. Pete's truck was gone, too, because he was at work.

Just as well. After the debacle with Emma, he wasn't fit company. He was hungry, too, damn it. Seemed like as upset as he was, he shouldn't feel like eating anything. But he could use a sandwich and a beer.

After parking the truck down by the barn, he walked back to the house, took his duffle into his bedroom and tossed it on the bed. Later. He'd bought sandwich fixings on Monday and left them for his dad and Pete. Should be some left.

Bingo. Plenty still in the fridge. He did most of the food shopping because he enjoyed the Eagles Nest Market and talking to Otto. On Monday, Otto had asked about Emma and Josh. He'd been pleased about the upcoming trip.

Putting down the sharp knife before he cut his damned self, Gage closed his eyes and braced his hands against the edge of the counter. But closing his eyes was worse. All he could see was Emma's tense expression and Josh's worried baby stare.

He'd thought he was good for them, that having him around was a bonus. Not this morning, not after he'd come up with an idea that had upset Emma and exposed how fragile their connection was. He'd been kidding himself that they were creating a strong connection.

After finishing the sandwich, he decided eating it in the house wouldn't work for him. Too confining. Ditto the porch. Grabbing his phone, he texted Pete and got permission to take Clifford for the afternoon.

Pete added a comment. *Thought you'd be in Great Falls until tomorrow. Everything OK?*

He held the phone and debated his answer. But there was no dodging this. Big party on Friday night. Whoever hadn't heard by then would figure out in five minutes there was an issue. He quickly typed *No* and turned off his phone.

Fifteen minutes later he had a good horse under him, grub and a couple of beers in the saddle bag and a sunny afternoon. Kendra had given him carte blanche to ride on Wild Creek Ranch land, so he headed over there.

Evidently he'd timed it perfectly. The open area between the house and the barn was empty and no riding lessons were going on in the corral. Folks were either running errands in town or taking a lunch break. He made it out the gate that led to open country without encountering a soul.

Once he reached a treeless expanse with nobody in sight, he nudged Clifford into a canter. Then he gave that big red horse his head. "Let 'er rip, buddy." He leaned over Clifford's neck and held onto his hat as the gelding stretched out, his pounding hoofs the loudest sound in the meadow.

Oh, yeah, this was exactly what he needed. And oh, yeah, he was getting himself a horse. Maybe even tomorrow.

He hadn't consciously chosen a destination, but after a reviving gallop that helped clear the cobwebs, he picked a trail and followed it. No surprise it was the same one Zane used when he released birds of prey found in this area. It ended at the edge of a wooded canyon that created updrafts perfect for an eagle or hawk launched back into the wild.

Leaving Clifford to graze on what was left of the summer grass, Gage unpacked his lunch and ate it while sitting on a fallen log at the edge of the drop-off. Somewhere along the line he'd stopped making these solo treks into wild country.

If you're very quiet, you can hear the Earth breathe.

His mom had said that to him once, probably to get him to be still and stop screwing around. But there was a rhythm to the wind through the tops of the trees that was like breathing. And a subtle echo in the canyon below. His tension slowly eased.

He needed more of this. More of—oh, hey, a pair of eagles soared overhead, executing dips and dives that would make a stunt pilot weep with envy. Too bad Josh wasn't here to see it.

But he would be, someday. That was nonnegotiable. A relationship with Emma might not work out. But he would by God share this kind of experience with Josh.

The longer he sat there, the more birds showed up. Next time he'd bring his binoculars, because he couldn't positively ID all of them. He lost track of how long he'd been there.

When he finally turned his phone back on, it was nearly dinnertime and he had a message. He wanted it to be Emma. Instead it was Pete. *We're home and Dad brought barbeque and coleslaw from the GG. Better get here before we eat it all. Oh, and Clifford wants his supper.*

On my way.

He was ready to face them, now. Clifford was motivated to get back to his cozy stall and the hay flake that would be waiting for him. They made good time.

Pete was down at the barn when he rode in. His big brother had already hauled out the grooming tote, a halter and a lead rope.

Gage swung down from the saddle. "Hey, bro. Figured you'd be up at the house noshing on barbeque."

"That was just to get your ass moving in this direction. We waited for you."

"Thanks. Appreciate the loan of your horse. I won't be needing him again." He tethered Clifford to the hitching post.

"Why not?"

"Starting tomorrow, I'll be looking for a horse."

"Will you, now?" Pete's eyebrows arched. "Thought that was a someday proposition."

"Someday has arrived."

"Alrighty, then." Pete didn't ask any questions or try to make conversation as they worked together brushing Clifford and putting away tack.

Neither did Gage. He'd rather save it for the dinner table.

By the time they walked into the house, their dad had everything set out, along with a beer at each place. He glanced at Gage. "Glad you could join us, son."

"Yeah, well..." He heaved a sigh. "Stuff happens." He and Pete washed up and took their usual chairs on opposite sides of the square table.

"Like I just told Pete, I'll be looking for a horse tomorrow, Dad. Don't know if you have time to go horse shopping, but I'd love to have you along."

His father gazed at him. "And I'd love to tag along. But if you decide to leave Eagles Nest, the horse goes with you."

"Who said I was leaving?"

"Nobody. And I hope you don't, but—"

"You think it's a possibility." *How invested are you in that town?*

His dad sighed. "I love you, son, however you choose to live your life. But up to now you've been a drifter. I think I know why and I've held out hope that eventually you'll find peace and settle down. Maybe this horse will be a start."

"A drifter? That's how you see me?" He looked at his dad, and then at Pete.

Pete shrugged. "You have to admit you don't stick around anywhere for long, bro."

"That's true, but—"

"There's no judgment in my saying it, son. If staying loose makes you happy, great. I'm not sure it does, though."

He pushed aside his plate, no longer hungry. "As it happens, staying loose sucks."

His dad's voice was gentle. "Care to talk about it?"

"Not much to tell. Everything was going fine with Emma and Josh. So this morning I asked if she'd consider moving to Eagles Nest." He took a ragged breath. "She turned me down flat. Evidently she sees me the way you do."

"She might. But the significant part for me is that you asked her to move here. How come?"

"Because I want to be with her. Her and Josh. I don't like having them four hours away."

His dad smiled. "Hallelujah. You have no idea how happy I am to hear you say that."

"Hey, bro, if she won't move here, you could move to Great Falls."

"She might not want me to, but even if she did, I'd rather make Eagles Nest my home base." He glanced at his dad. "I don't know what finding peace means, exactly, but I do feel more settled here, like this is where I'm supposed to be."

"But it sounds like you didn't tell her that."

"No, I didn't. I don't quite trust that feeling enough to say something so..."

"Revealing?"

Bullseye. "Yeah."

"When you do feel ready, a discussion with Emma might have a whole different outcome."

"I doubt she feels like discussing anything with me at this point. As they say, actions speak louder than words. I don't think talking's going to fix this."

"Then you'll have to come up with something else, won't you?"

"Right." He held his dad's gaze. Then he pushed back his chair and stood. "If you two will excuse me, I'm going to take my beer and engage in a little porch sitting. I have some cogitating to do."

"Take your time, son."

"I will, Dad." The evening breeze had a nip to it. Fine with him. Made his brain work better. Moving a rocker to the railing, he sat down and put his feet up.

Up to now you've been a drifter. I think I know why.

He let the words soak in. Closed his eyes. He hadn't looked at the family albums in years, but he didn't have to for one image to be clear as a bell. His mom, her curly dark hair blowing in the breeze, was pouring seed into a birdfeeder while he stood beside her, a little dude of about four, helping his mom feed the sparrows. He hadn't been a drifter then.

No, he'd stuck real close. He was in most of the pictures of her, just like Pete was in most of the ones of his dad.

But if your mother can be taken, nothing is safe. Better to stay loose. His throat ached. He squeezed his eyes shut, fighting the grief, but the hot tears dribbled out, anyway. *Damn it, why did you have to die? Why couldn't you be here to see my son? To see how cool he is? He has your eyes...*

Gulping, he yanked his bandanna out of his pocket and mopped his face. Then he leaned his head back and took a long, slow breath. Calmer, now.

I think I know why. Wise man, his dad.

What would his mom say about how he'd conducted himself so far? She'd tell him to think about all the things he had instead of what he'd lost. And he had a bucketful of blessings, Josh being the newest and most precious. But he also had Pete, Wes, Roxanne and his dad.

I've held out hope that eventually you'll find peace.

Maybe he did have some grasp on that concept. His best chance was here—a new start in a new town, with his family around him. And Kendra, who'd brought joy to his dad and had swept the Sawyer kids under her wing. She'd be as much of a mother to him as he'd allow.

She was such a giving woman. She'd leaped to organize the birthday party and she'd offered Emma and Josh a place to stay during the weekend. Which was awesome of her because this house wasn't big enough, except...

Emma and Josh should stay with him whenever they came down. He was the daddy. Looked like he needed a house of his own, now, didn't it? A house with a barn. Yeah, he should have a place to stable his own damn horse and not count on his father to provide a stall.

Oh, and he might want to get a *job* while he was at it. And this just in—not wrangling horses, either. The idea hit him like a lightning bolt. He wanted to work for Zane at Raptors Rise.

Zane might not have a paying position right now, but he'd work for free if necessary and apply for a bartending job to make ends meet. God, he'd love working at the rescue center. Why hadn't he thought of it before?

Because he'd had his head up his butt, that's why. Consequently, he might have ruined his chances with Emma. Or maybe not. Either way,

his drifting days were over. It was time to grow
the hell up.

27

Emma couldn't catch a break. The country music station she'd found as she approached Eagles Nest had a DJ who seemed determined to play love song after love song, each one designed to rip her heart out and stomp all over it.

But with Josh awake and restless after the long drive, she needed to entertain him. He also expected her to sing along, and the lyrics were killing her. Then, as she approached the turnoff for the dirt road leading to Wild Creek Ranch, the guy finally cued up something that wasn't about effing love—*Boot Scootin' Boogie.*

Dear God, what had she done to deserve this torture? But she valiantly belted out the words for Josh's sake while he rocked and giggled in his car seat. Happy baby. Miserable mommy.

She was grateful that he hadn't seemed to miss Gage too much. He'd be excited to see his daddy again, though. She, on the other hand, battled a mixture of dread and yearning.

The Wild Creek Ranch sign was decorated with balloons and a hand-lettered sign that said *Happy First Birthday, Josh!* She drove past it, pulled over and got out to take a picture.

Oh, man, was that Gage's truck right behind her? What were the chances? He pulled over, too, and got out. The rat was wearing the same damn mascara shirt. And looking his usual broad-shouldered, lean-hipped, gorgeous self.

But as he approached, the cocky grin was missing. "Hello, Emma."

"Hello, Gage." She was breathing way too fast. She wasn't as prepared for this face-to-face as she would have liked. Hyperventilating and passing out at his feet would not be cool. "Fancy meeting you here."

"Kendra told me when she was expecting you. I waited across the road and followed you in. I counted on you stopping to take a picture of the sign."

"Guess I'm predictable."

"You're a great mom who wants plenty of pictures to show Josh when he's older. Listen, I wanted to ask you something before we're surrounded by a bunch of people."

She hesitated before responding. The last time he'd started a conversation like that, he'd blindsided her. "Okay." Breathing was still a major effort, but it helped that he seemed to be having the same problem.

"Since the party's breaking up about eight, I was hoping you'd agree to take a drive with me afterward. I've cleared it with Kendra. She'll be happy to watch Josh."

"I think I should stay and help clean up after all that she's done."

"She figured you might say that. She wanted me to assure you that it's more important to her that you go with me."

"She knows what this is all about?"

"Yes."

"Does everybody at the party know?"

"Most of them."

"Why not just tell me now and save time?"

"Because I want your undivided attention. And I don't want to encroach on Josh's birthday celebration."

She might be making a mistake, but she owed it to Josh to hear whatever his daddy had to say. "Then it's a date."

"Thank you." He touched the brim of his hat. "See you up at the house. Don't want to keep Josh staring at the upholstery any longer." He jogged back to his truck.

She hurried to the car and climbed in.

"Da-da!" Josh crowed from the back seat.

"Yes, baby boy. That certainly was your daddy." She blew out a breath and pulled onto the road. "And he's up to something."

Gage followed her to the house and parked next to her, but they'd no sooner exited their vehicles than Quinn and Kendra came down the porch steps, followed by the Sawyer clan. No wonder Gage had waylaid her at the turnoff. They'd have no chance to talk now.

"I'll get Josh, if that's okay," Gage said.

"Sure, that's fine." She pulled out her suitcase and Josh's baby backpack.

"I've got those." Quinn hurried over and gave her a quick kiss on the cheek. "Good to have you back."

"Thanks, I—"

"Emma." Kendra hugged her tight. "Did Gage give you my message?"

"He did."

"You going?"

"Yes."

"Great. Now I'll get out of the way so the rest of your fan club can say hi."

"Emma!" Roxanne came toward her, arms outstretched.

She got a little choked up as she collected more hugs from Ingrid, Michael, Pete and Wes. They had to know that Gage's visit to Great Falls had ended on a sour note. Evidently that wasn't going to stop them from treating her as a cherished member of the family.

She glanced up at the porch. "The place looks fabulous." Cardboard cutouts of birds hung from the rafters along with various birthday greetings and birthday-themed garlands.

"Dad and I hit a party store in Bozeman," Roxanne said. "I was so happy they had cutouts of birds."

"So is the birthday boy." Emma followed Gage's progress as he carried Josh up the steps. The kid was babbling away like crazy and pointing to the cutouts swinging in the breeze.

Roxanne smiled. "Just the reaction we were going for."

When Emma finally made it into the house, she was greeted by the other four members of the Whine and Cheese Club, who'd clearly been organizing things in the kitchen. Not long after that, Kendra's family arrived bringing warm hugs, welcoming smiles and gifts.

The pile on the dining room table grew. How long would it take to open all those, and would everything fit in her car?

Kendra must have seen her eyeing the stash because she pulled her aside. "I told everyone that with so many gifts, we'd wait and open them later. Is that okay?"

"Excellent idea. Then I can make a proper list for thank you cards."

"And we won't be here all night."

Emma chuckled. "That, too."

"You don't have to take them all home this weekend, either. I'll store some for you."

"Thanks. It's—"

"Overwhelming. I know."

"But so sweet and generous. I'll never forget this."

The mountain of presents was only rivaled by the amount of food, which was served buffet-style in the kitchen. People carried loaded plates to wherever they found a spot—in the living room and out on the wide front porch.

The huge cake that followed, a snowy masterpiece created by Ingrid and Abigail, was decorated with, of course, birds. Emma took at least a dozen pictures of Josh's wide eyes as Gage held him close enough to see, but not close enough to touch.

The birthday song was enthusiastically rendered. Then phones came out as Gage, Emma and Josh worked together to blow out the single candle at the top of the cake.

After the cake was cut and everyone had a piece, Quinn set the high chair on a drop cloth in the middle of the living room. Gage slid Josh into it, Emma put on his bib and Kendra came over with a small piece of cake.

She laid the cake directly on the tray of the high chair. "It's cake, Josh."

"Kuk-kuk?"

"Cake."

He stared at it for a moment, poked it with his finger and put his finger in his mouth. His grin was something to behold. "Kuk-kuk!" Using both hands, he attacked the cake until he was covered with it.

A bunch of people were taking videos, so Emma chose not to. Watching was more fun, anyway. *Taking a video in my head* as Gage had phrased it.

He came over to stand beside her. "Kendra had an idea. Folks will be leaving soon, so if we tell Josh we're taking a drive and go out on the porch, we can say goodbye to everyone as they walk out. Then after they're all gone, we can leave."

"But Josh is a mess. I need to—"

"She and Dad would love to give him his bath. To hear them talk, bath time was a highlight during the night they babysat."

Mention of that night flooded her with memories and she glanced quickly toward the porch, as if considering the plan. "Okay, then. Let's do that."

The party had distracted her somewhat, but his request to spend time alone with her had created a low hum of tension beneath the laughter and happy chatter. Heaven help her, she wanted to spend time alone with him. She wanted to hear what he had to say. But she wouldn't get her hopes up and she'd stay on her guard.

She gave Josh a kiss on his sticky cheek and said she'd be back soon. Gage did the same and walked with her out to the porch. Thanking everyone as they left was just plain fun. She loved this cheerful, flag-football-playing bunch and would be putting a lot of miles on her SUV in the future.

"What a great party." Roxanne came out the door with Michael and walked over to give Emma a hug. "Love that little booger."

"He sure hit the jackpot today." Emma smiled. "Thank you both for coming."

"Wouldn't miss it." Michael gave her a hug and shook hands with Gage. "By the way, buddy, I checked on our current work assignments, so give me a call when you have a chance."

"Will do, Michael. Thanks."

"Oh, and we're the tail end of the parade," Roxanne said. "Dad wanted me to be sure and tell you that."

Which meant it was time for that drive with Gage. Emma's stomach did a little flip-flop.

"Thanks, sis." Gage gave Roxanne a hug.

"Welcome." She murmured something in his ear that sounded like *good luck.* Then she and Michael went down the steps and out to the parking area.

Emma turned to Gage. "Did she wish you good luck?"

"Yes, ma'am."

"What's going—"

"You'll see in a little bit. Let's vamoose."

"All right." She walked with him down the steps. "It sounds like you applied for a job at the Guzzling Grizzly."

"I did. Michael's ready to hire me. We just have to figure out which shifts I'll cover." When they reached his truck, he handed her into the cab.

"But I thought you wanted ranch work."

"I'll explain on the way." He closed the door, went around to the driver's side and climbed behind the wheel. "I changed my mind about hiring on somewhere as a wrangler." He started the truck and backed out. "Instead I'll be working with Zane over at Raptor's Rise."

"Really? That's wonderful!"

"Yeah, it is." He switched on the headlights and started down the dirt road. "He can't pay much, which is why I'm going to moonlight for a while at the GG. But if I'm at the center fulltime, that allows him to do more outreach to increase funding. He's ready to grow the operation and I'll be a part of that."

"I'm excited for you. Even better, you sound excited."

"I've never been this gung-ho about a job. Think of what I'll learn! And I'll be helping those birds heal and get back to the life they were meant for."

She studied his profile in the light from the dash. Something was different about him. The change was subtle, though. He'd always cultivated a nonchalant expression, but now he looked genuinely relaxed. Yet purposeful. It was a sexy combo.

He turned left onto the paved road. "We're not far from where I want to take you, but before we get there, I need to apologize for that half-assed suggestion that you move to Eagles Nest. I wasn't looking at it from your angle. No wonder you rejected the idea."

"It did come out of the blue."

"And I didn't acknowledge all that you've done to create a good environment for Josh—babyproofing the house, adding a swing and a sandbox, plus the birdfeeder. Like I said, I'm sorry."

"Apology accepted." He'd clearly spent time thinking about it. Maybe he was beginning to understand.

He put on his left turn signal.

"Are we going off-road? I see a break in the fence, but no—"

"There's a road here, but it needs work. Hang on."

She gripped the dash as the truck bounced over a rutted, barely-there road. It ended in a clearing and the headlights illuminated the front of a house.

"This is it."

"This is what?"

"My house."

"*Your* house? Since when did you—"

"Since yesterday, although technically it's not mine yet. Deidre worked some magic and got me the keys. She's trusting me to give them back tomorrow because this isn't kosher." He opened the console and took out a flashlight. "Better stay there and let me come around. The ground's uneven." He shut off the headlights and got out.

He had a *house*? Talk about surreal.

After he helped her down, he kept hold of her hand and turned on the flashlight. "Despite the terrible road, the house is in pretty good shape. It belonged to an introverted guy who spit-shined the house but didn't want visitors." He shifted the beam of light over to the left. "The barn's not in bad condition, either, although he didn't use it."

"Do you need a barn?"

"Yep. For my horse. One of the horses boarded at Kendra's is for sale and he might be perfect for me. I just need to take him out on the trail a few more times to make sure we suit each other, but we had a great ride yesterday."

"Wow. Are all these changes since Wednesday, or were some of them in the works and you just didn't tell me?"

"All since Wednesday, but they've been due for a long, long time." He squeezed her hand and started for the house. "Let me show you the inside."

"Okay." He'd accomplished more in forty-eight hours than most people would in a month. She was more than a little curious where all this was leading as she climbed the porch steps.

Releasing her hand, he trained the flashlight on the door and inserted the key in the lock. "There we go." Opening it wide, he led her through the doorway.

"No electricity?"

"Not turned on. I know it's hard to see with just a flashlight." He swept the beam around the empty room. "There's moonlight coming through the windows. That'll help. The fireplace is pretty." He drew her to the far side of the room and trained the light on a rock fireplace.

"Very nice. But I'm kerflummoxed. What's going on?" And this time she'd make sure she got some answers.

"Everything." He glanced at the moonlight spilling through a large picture window. "I'm gonna douse this." He turned off the flashlight and laid it on the mantle. "The moon's nicer." Then he gazed at her. "Now that we're here, I don't know where to start."

"Start with this house. Why did you buy it and why so fast?"

"I had to buy it fast because someone else was extremely interested and I didn't want to let it get away. As to why I need a house, it's for me, because it's high time I had my own place."

"How big is it? I couldn't really tell when we were outside."

"Three bedrooms, two baths, twenty-five-hundred square feet."

"That's a big house for one person."

"You sound suspicious."

"Because I am. I hope you didn't buy this because—"

"I didn't buy this with the idea you and Josh would live in it, if that's what you're thinking. But I do hope you'll agree to stay here when you come down for a visit."

"Instead of at Wild Creek Ranch?"

"Exactly. As you probably noticed, this place is only a couple of miles down the road from Kendra's, and from my dad's house, too, so they could still see a lot of Josh. But he's my son. If you'll agree to it, I want him—and you—to stay with me. I'd like this to be Josh's second home. I've already figured out where I could put a sandbox and a swing."

The image brought a lump to her throat, but she pushed it down. She had to be strong, for Josh. "Come on, Gage. I can't believe you didn't buy this place hoping we'd live here eventually."

"I wouldn't be human if I didn't have some hope of that."

"Aha! I—"

"But I won't bring it up. That's a promise. If you should want to discuss it sometime in the future, I'm all ears. For now, the subject's closed."

She stared at him. He'd actually figured it out. "I'm stunned."

"Why?"

"Three days ago, you had no concrete plan for the future. Since you left Great Falls, you've thrown in with Zane's operation—which is a fabulous idea, by the way—you're in escrow for this house and you're ready to buy a horse."

"Yes, ma'am."

"Was my comment about putting down roots the catalyst?" If so, they could still be on shaky ground.

"Not exactly. It was what my dad said. He called me a drifter. Not in a mean way, just calmly stating a fact. I didn't like it. I especially didn't like it because he was right."

"That had to be tough to hear." Her heart ached for him.

"It's what I needed to hear, though. I've committed to changing, for Josh's sake, but mostly for my own. I'll do whatever it takes to break that pattern. If I don't, I'll cheat myself out of the good stuff."

She moved closer, needing contact. "Like your relationship with Josh?"

"Yep. And...with you. I've done a great job of mucking that up, but I—"

"Maybe that can change, too." She took another step. He was only inches away. His body heat called to her and his uneven breathing sent a shiver of anticipation up her spine.

"I sure hope that's true, because it's the other reason I wanted a chance to talk with you. It wasn't just to show you the house."

"No?" She eliminated the distance between them so her body brushed his.

"I've discovered something, and I think it's only fair to tell you. I mean, it seems like something you should know, since it concerns you."

"What?" The shadows hid his expression.

"I'm in love with you."

Her breath caught. "You are?"

"Head-over-heels, crazy as a loon in love with you." Sliding his arms around her waist, he drew her gently into his arms. "What do you think of that?"

She gulped. "I'm...even more stunned."

"So am I. I've never said that to a woman before. Was nervous about saying it to you. But it feels damned good to get it out. I love you, Emma. I love you."

Her heart was beating so fast she was light-headed. "Well, in that case…" She paused to clear her throat. "I should probably tell you something."

"I'm listening." He sounded apprehensive.

"Turns out I'm in love with you, too."

His grip tightened. "You're kidding."

"Nope." She swallowed. "I would never kid about that. What do you think?"

"That I'm dreaming this."

"You're not." She pinched him lightly on the ear. "Now what do you think?"

His voice was thick with emotion. "That I'm the luckiest bastard in the universe." Capturing her mouth, he kissed the daylights out of her until the need to breathe forced him to stop for a minute. "You love me? You're sure?"

Heart racing, she cradled his face in both hands. "I. Love. You."

"I can't get my head around it. I can't—"

"Here's an idea." She pulled him down until their lips almost touched. "Just keep kissing me. Eventually maybe it will sink in."

"Could take a while." There was a hint of laughter in his voice.

"You got somewhere to go?"

"No ma'am. I'm exactly where I want to be."

His words had special meaning, now. "So am I, Gage. So am I." Giddy with joy, she surrendered to the magic of his kiss and the warmth of his loving arms.

Pete Sawyer faces pure temptation in the form of guest ranch owner Taryn Maroney, who also happens to be his employer, in A COWBOY'S HOLIDAY, book twelve in the McGavin Brothers series!

* * * * *

"This ranch is the most important thing in my life right now."

And he was part of that. Good enough. Pete looped the end of the light strand around a branch so it would stay put. "Then I guess it's important that you came up here with me, so you can get a really great view of it." He raised the crane's bucket to its maximum height and swiveled it so Taryn was facing away from the trees. "Take a look. There's your ranch."

She gave a little gasp of delight. "It's *beautiful* from up here. Can you see how gracefully the buildings are nestled in the trees?"

"Yep. You get a real appreciation of that from here."

"Even better, the cabins I added flow with the rest of the buildings. They look as if they've been there all along. I planned it that way, but now that I see it laid out from this vantage point...it really works."

"It does. You've done a great job."

"You know how I'd like to commemorate this moment up here with you?"

A kiss? Did he dare hope? "How?"

"Take a selfie of the two of us."

He quickly downgraded his expectations. "Sure, why not?"

"Could you please take it?" She held out her phone. "You have longer arms."

"I'll do my best. I'm no expert at this, though. I've done it maybe twice." He pulled off his gloves, shoved them in his pocket and took her phone. "You'll have to coach me."

"First we need to get closer." She moved in next to him, nudging the empty light boxes out of the way. Then she wrapped her arm around his waist and snuggled in.

He could do no less than put his arm around her waist and nestle her against him. Selfies rocked. "Now what?"

"Click that little symbol in the bottom right corner so the camera focuses on us."

He managed that, and there they were in the frame, Taryn smiling and looking adorable in her hard hat, him looking...dazed and confused, but happy.

"Bring your head down next to mine so our cheeks are almost touching. That's better."

Certainly was.

"Now put your thumb on the shutter in the middle and smile." She kept her smile in place while she said that, which had to be a learned skill. He couldn't talk and smile at the same time.

A happy face was easy, though, when her warm body was tucked in close and her spicy scent tickled his nose. He tapped the button with his thumb.

"I don't think that took. I didn't hear the squeal-click."

"Squeal-click?" He looked at her. "What's that?"

She turned her head, which brought her very, very close. She swallowed and her eyelashes fluttered. "The noise it makes when…it takes a picture." Her gaze dropped to his mouth.

"Oh."

Her voice grew breathy. "You must not…take many pictures."

"I don't." His heart thudded with almost painful intensity.

Then she slowly closed her eyes.

Yes. He had to tilt his head to avoid a hard-hat collision, but he was motivated. Once he had the angle right, the space between his lips and hers disappeared as if by magic. He touched down and she whimpered. He increased the pressure and she moaned.

Or maybe that was him. He lost track. Her lips parted, inviting him in, blocking out everything but the heat, the fire, and a high-pitched whirring noise….

*New York Times bestselling author Vicki Lewis
Thompson's love affair with cowboys started with
the Lone Ranger, continued through Maverick, and
took a turn south of the border with Zorro. She
views cowboys as the Western version of knights in
shining armor, rugged men who value honor,
honesty and hard work. Fortunately for her, she
lives in the Arizona desert, where broad-shouldered,
lean-hipped cowboys abound. Blessed with such an
abundance of inspiration, she only hopes that she
can do them justice.*

*For more information about this prolific author,
visit her website and sign up for her newsletter. She
loves connecting with readers.*

VickiLewisThompson.com